PATH IN

Katherine Saffery.
Class 3F.

1983.

George Dixon School
46, Olmestary Road
Moseley
B'ham B13 8LE

Other Science-Fiction Anthologies in Pan

THE SEVENTH GALAXY READER

THE EIGHTH GALAXY READER

STAR FOURTEEN

SPECTRUM V

A CENTURY OF SCIENCE FICTION

PATH INTO THE UNKNOWN

The Best Soviet Science Fiction

UNABRIDGED

PAN BOOKS LTD : LONDON

First published 1966 by MacGibbon and Kee Ltd.,
This edition published 1969 by Pan Books Ltd.,
33 Tothill Street, London, S.W.1

330 02353 5

MacGibbon and Kee wish to acknowledge the assistance of the Novosti Publishing House (APN) without whose help this collection would not have been possible.

Printed and Bound in England by
Hazell Watson & Viney Ltd.,
Aylesbury, Bucks

CONTENTS

Ilya Varshavsky

To Stanislav Lemm, in memory of our argument which will never be resolved.

THE CONFLICT

'H-M, it looks as if we've been crying? Why? Has anything happened?'

Martha removed her husband's hand from beneath her chin, and, her head drooping, said:

'Nothing. I simply felt blue.'

'Anything to do with Eric?'

'Oh, no. He's an ideal child. A worthy product of a machine upbringing. With a nannie like her, Eric will never give his parents any trouble.'

'He's asleep?'

'He's being told the usual bedtime story. I went in ten minutes ago. He was sitting in his cot, his face flushed, casting adoring glances at his beloved Cybella. Didn't even notice me at first. But when I came up to give him a kiss he waved me away with both little hands, as if to tell me to wait until the story ended. Of course a mother's not an electronic machine, she can wait.'

'What did Cybella do?'

'Charming, clever, level-headed Cybella was up to the mark as she always is. "Eric," she says, "give your mother, with whom you have a blood bond, a good night kiss. What did I tell you about chromosome division?"'

'Why do you hate Cybella so?'

Martha's eyes filled with tears.

'I can't stand it any longer, Luff! Please understand! Always feeling that rational machine's superiority at every step! Hardly a day passes without her letting me realize my inferiority. Please do something, do! Why do those awful machines have to be so horribly intelligent? Can't they perform their tasks without that? Who needs that?'

'It happens of its own accord. The laws of self-organization are responsible. We have no hand in it whether it's individual traits or, regrettably, even genius. Want me to ask for another robot in Cybella's place?'

'Unfortunately, that's out of the question. Eric simply dotes on her. Better do something to it to make it a bit stupider. Then I'd find it much easier.'

'But that'd be a crime! Don't you know that the law has made thinking robots man's equal?'

'Talk to her then! She told me such a terrible thing today that I was even at a loss what to say. No, I simply can't stand this humiliation any longer!'

'Quiet, she's coming! Get yourself in hand!'

'Hullo, boss!'

'Why that, Cybella? Surely you know the A-1 machine doesn't use that word.'

'Well, you see, I thought Martha would like it. She is always only too delighted to stress the difference between the lord of creation and a man-made machine.'

Martha put up a hankie to her eyes and rushed out of the room.

'Is that all?' Cybella asked.

'Yes, you may go.'

Some ten minutes later Luff went into the kitchen.

'What are you doing at the moment, Cybella?'

With measured movements Cybella removed a spool of microfilm from the receptacle in her temple.

'I was studying up Flemish painting. It's my day off tomorrow and I'd like to see my descendant. His teachers say he has a genius for drawing. But I'm afraid he will not get a good enough art training at the boarding school. I have to make up for that on my days off.'

'What happened between you and Martha today?'

'Nothing special. I was clearing up the table in the morning, when by pure chance I caught a glimpse of one of the pages in her thesis and happened to notice two essential errors in the formula for the nucleic acid code. It would have been stupid of me not to tell Martha about it. I simply wanted to help her.'

'And what happened?'

'She started crying and said she was a live human being, not a robot and that to have a machine lecturing her all the time, was just as repulsive to her as kissing a "fridge".'

'You, of course, answered back?'

'Yes, I said that if she could gratify her progenitive instinct with the help of a fridge, she would probably see nothing reprehensible in kissing it.'

'I see. But it wasn't very nice to mention the instinct business.'

'I didn't want to hurt her. I simply wanted her to realize that it was all so very relative.'

'Please be a bit more tactful with Martha. She is so very high strung.'

'Yes, boss.'

Luff winced and took himself off to the bedroom.

Martha was asleep, her nose pressed into the pillow, and whimpering from time to time.

Trying not to waken her, Luff tiptoed away and lay down on the couch.

He felt terrible.

Meanwhile in the kitchen Cybella thought that this constant contact with human beings was growing unbearable, that one could not demand machines that were now much cleverer than man to express everlasting gratitude to their creators, and that if not for maternal affection for her little cyberkid, who had no one else in the whole wide world, she would willingly throw herself out of the twentieth floor window.

Ilya Varshavsky

ROBBY

SEVERAL months ago I celebrated my fiftieth birthday.

After numerous toasts praising my merits and glossing over my inherent faults, radionics laboratory chief Strekozov rose, glass in hand, to say:

'Now our laboratory's youngest representative will greet the hero of the occasion.'

For some reason everyone glanced at the door.

In the silence that set in, a scratching on the door could be heard. Then the door opened and a robot rolled in.

Everyone applauded.

'This robot,' Strekozov went on, 'is a self-teaching automatic machine. It has no prescribed programme, drafting its own programme to suit the changing circumstances. Stored in its memory are more than a thousand words. What's more its vocabulary keeps on growing. It can freely read a printed text, compose sentences and understand human speech. It runs on storage batteries which it recharges itself from the mains whenever necessary. We spent a whole year working evenings to present it to you on your birthday. It can be taught to perform any task.

'Now Robby,' he said, addressing the robot, 'say hullo to your new master.'

Robby rolled up to me and uttered, after a slight pause:

'It will give me pleasure if you will be happy to accept me as a member of your family.'

He put it very nicely – even though I didn't think it so well phrased.

Everyone crowded around Robby to get a better look at him.

'We can't have him walking around the apartment stark naked,' my mother-in-law said. 'I'll sew him a Mother Hubbard.'

Waking up next morning I found Robby by my bedside apparently awaiting instructions. It was a most exciting moment.

'Be so kind, Robby, as to shine my shoes,' I said. 'They are standing in the hallway at the door.'

'How does one shine shoes?' he asked.

'It's all very simple. In the locker you'll find some brown shoe polish and a couple of brushes. Spread the polish on and rub it in with a brush until the shoes shine.'

Robby obediently made for the hallway.

I was extremely curious to see how he would cope with his first task.

When I came up he had just finished spreading over my shoes the apricot jam my wife was saving for a very special occasion.

'Oh, Robby,' I said, 'I forgot to tell you that the shoe polish is on the lower shelf. You took the wrong jar.'

'The spatial position of any object,' he said imperturbably watching me try to clean my shoes of the mess, 'may be given by three co-ordinates in Descartes' system of co-ordinates. The allowance may not exceed the object's dimensions.'

'Quite right, Robby, I was mistaken.'

'Any point in space, in particular the corner of this room, could be taken as the starting point for the co-ordinates required.'

'Yes, I understand all that, I'll take it into consideration in the future.'

'The co-ordinates of an object may also be given in angular dimensions by means of azimuth and altitude,' he continued in his rasping voice.

'All right, all right, forget it.'

'The tolerated allowance in the case in question,

considering the ratio between the object's dimensions and the length of the radius vector, should not exceed two-thousandths of a radian by azimuth and one-thousandth of a radian by altitude.'

'Enough!' I exclaimed in anger. 'Stop talking about it.'

He indeed stopped talking, but spent the whole day following in my footsteps, trying to explain to me by gestures the singularities involved in switching from a right-angle system to an oblique as in right-angle system of co-ordinates.

Frankly speaking I felt worn to a shred before the day ended.

I soon realized that Robby was more suited for intellectual work than manual labour, very unwillingly undertaking anything prosaic. To be fair, though, I must say he was a wizard at numbers.

My wife says that if not for his mania of reckoning everything with an accuracy down to the thousandth of a kopeck, the help he gives in tallying household expenses would be invaluable.

My wife and mother-in-law are convinced Robby is a great mathematician. I, on the other hand, think his knowledge very superficial.

At tea time one day my wife said:

'Robby, get the cake from the kitchen, slice it into three portions and serve it.'

'That can't be done,' he said after a brief period of reflection.

'But why?'

'Because a unit cannot be divided into three parts. The result of such division is a circulating decimal which cannot be calculated with unerring accuracy.'

My wife gave me a helpless look.

'I think Robby is right,' my mother-in-law said. 'I seem to have heard about that before.'

'Robby,' I said, 'this is not a problem of the arithmetical

division of a unit into three parts, but the division of a geometric figure into three equivalent areas. The cake is round, so if you divide the circumference into three parts and draw radii from the points of division, you will thus be able to divide the cake into three equal parts.'

'Nonsense!' he retorted with obvious annoyance. 'To divide a circumference into three parts, I must first know the length, which is the product of the diameter times the surd "pi". This problem is impossible to solve as, in the final analysis, it represents a variation of the problem of squaring the circle.'

'Quite right!' my mother-in-law seconded. 'We learned that back at school. One day our maths master, whom we all adored, entered the classroom ...'

'Please excuse me for butting in,' I again intervened, 'but there are several ways of dividing a circumference into three parts and if, Robby, you come with me to the kitchen, I'll show you how it's done.'

'I cannot have somebody with thought processes restricted in velocity teaching me what to do,' he challengingly retorted.

Even my wife couldn't take that lying down. She doesn't like it when strangers question my mental capacities.

'You should be ashamed of yourself, Robby!'

'I can't hear you, I can't hear you,' he rumbled demonstratively switching off the tumbler of the sound receptor.

Our first quarrel began with a trifle. At dinner one day, I related the following joke:

'One travelling salesman meets another on a steamer.'

'"Where are you going?" he asks.

'"To Odessa," the second replies.

'"Now you say you're going to Odessa, so that I think you're not going there. However you are really going there, so why lie about it?"'

The joke was appreciated.

'Kindly repeat the initial data,' Robby spoke up.

Now though it's not very pleasant to tell the same story twice to one and the same audience, I reluctantly proceeded to do as requested. Robby said nothing. I knew he was able to perform around a thousand logical operations a minute and realized what a titanic effort he was making throughout this protracted period of silence.

'It's absurd,' he at last ejaculated. 'If he's really going to Odessa and says he is going there, then he isn't lying.'

'Quite right, Robby. But the joke's funny precisely because it is absurd.'

'Is everything that is absurd funny in that case?'

'No, not everything. But in this case you have a situation when the absurdity is funny.'

'Are there any algorithms for evolving such situations?'

'I really don't know, Robby. There are a vast number of funny jokes but nobody has ever approached them from that angle.'

'I see.'

I woke up at night with a jolt as somebody had gripped me by the shoulders and made me sit up. Robby confronted me.

'What on earth has happened?' I asked, rubbing my eyes.

'A says X equals Y, while B claims that X doesn't equal Y as Y equals X. Is that the gist of your joke?'

'I really don't know Robby. Now for God's sake, don't bother me with algorithms and let me go to sleep again.'

'There isn't any God,' Robby said, rolling off into his corner.

The next day, when we were at the table, Robby suddenly announced:

'I've got a joke I must tell you.'

'Fire away, Robby,' I said.

'A customer asks a sales clerk how much one unit of the commodity he is selling costs. The sales clerk says that one unit of the commodity he is selling costs one rouble. To that the customer says: "You say the price is one rouble, so that I think the price is not the same as one rouble. But the price is really equal to one rouble. Why are you lying?'

'What a nice joke,' my mother-in-law said. 'I'll have to remember it.'

'Why don't you laugh?' Robby asked.

'Well, you see, Robby,' I said, 'your joke isn't very funny. The situation isn't one that seems funny.'

'No, it is a funny joke,' Robby obstinately returned, 'and you've got to laugh.'

'But how can one laugh if it isn't funny?'

'But it is funny! I insist that you laugh! You must laugh! I demand that you laugh! Because it is funny I demand, prescribe, command you to laugh without delay, this very instant! Ha-ha-ha!'

Robby was clearly in a temper.

My wife placed her spoon on the table and turning to me, said:

'You never give us a chance to have dinner in quiet. Who are you trying to convince? Sending poor Robby into hysterics with your silly stupid jokes, indeed!'

Wiping her tears, she went out. My mother-in-law followed, her nose in the air, saying nothing.

Robby and I were left all alone.

That was when he went the whole hog!

The word 'stupid' uncorked a whole splurge of synonyms from his extended vocabulary.

'Dope!' he shouted at the top of his loudspeakers. 'Blockhead! Imbecile! Idiot! Lunatic! Moron! Neurotic! Laugh, you degenerate, because it is funny! X doesn't equal Y because Y equals X. Ha-ha-ha!'

I would prefer to refrain from relating the revolting things that happened further. I am afraid I wasn't able to behave like a real man. Bombarded with abuse and clenching my fists in impotent fury I broke into a cowardly giggle, trying to pacify the rampant robot.

'Laugh louder you nitwit!' He would not be appeased. 'Ha-ha-ha.'

The next day, the doctor ordered me to bed with high blood pressure.

Robby preened himself on his ability to identify visual images. He had a staggering visual memory which enabled him to recognize from among a hundred and one intricate patterns the one he had once but casually glimpsed.

I did my best to develop this ability.

In summer my wife left for her holiday, while my mother-in-law went to visit her son. Robby and I were left all alone in our flat.

'I needn't worry about you,' my wife said on parting. 'Robby will take good care of you. But don't you insult him.'

There being a heat wave at the time, I followed my customary practice of shaving my head.

Back from the barber's, I summoned Robby. He appeared at once.

'Robby be kind enough to give me dinner.'

'All the food in this flat and equally so all the articles therein contained, with the exception of objects of the municipal service, belong to its owner. I cannot comply with your demand, it being an attempt to appropriate the property of others.'

'But I am the owner of this flat.'

Robby stalked right up to me and scrutinized my person from head to foot.

'Your image does not correspond to the image of the owner of this flat as stored in my memory cells.'

'I've simply shaved my head, Robby, that's all. I myself haven't changed at all. Can't you recognize my voice?'

'A person's voice can be taped,' Robby dryly returned.

'But there are hundreds of other tokens to show that I am I. I always thought you capable of realizing such elementary things.'

'External images represent an objective reality that does not depend on one's perceptive faculties.'

His smug pomposity began to irritate me.

'I've long been planning to have a serious talk with you, Robby. I think it would be much more useful for you not to clutter up your memory with too intricate notions and give more attention to your main obligations.'

'Depart from these premises at once,' he commanded in a rattle. 'Depart, go, disappear, move off! Otherwise I shall employ with respect to you physical force, violence, coercion, blows, knocks, bruises, injuries.'

As ill-luck would have it, I knew that when Robby got into that vein, all arguing was futile.

To cap it I did not at all relish the prospect of being bashed in the face by him. He had quite a heavy hand.

I spent the next three weeks at my friend's place, returning home only after my wife had come back.

By that time an inch of hair had grown.

Robby feels quite at home in our flat. He spends every evening watching the telly. The rest of the time he narcissistically tinkers with his own set-up, loudly whistling some sort of a tune the while. Unfortunately he has no ear, his designer having failed to provide it.

I am afraid Robby's urge for self-perfection is assuming ugly forms. He does household chores most reluctantly and negligently. Everything that has no bearing on his own person he treats with obvious disdain, taking a patronising tone to everyone.

My wife tried to use him for translation from foreign languages. He learned the Franco-Russian dictionary off by rote with amazing ease and now avidly devours a mass of trashy paperbooks. Whenever asked to translate what he has read, he airily returns:

'It's absolutely uninteresting. Read it yourself.'

I have taught him chess. At first everything went swimmingly, but then a logical analysis evidently suggested that dishonest methods presented the surest way to a win.

He avails himself of every opportunity to surreptitiously re-arrange my figures.

Once, in the middle of a game I discovered that my king had vanished.

'What on earth have you done with my king, Robby?'

'I mated you at the third move and so removed your king,' he insolently declared.

'That's theoretically impossible. Mate is impossible in the first three moves. Put my king back.'

'There's a lot you've got to learn in chess,' he said, sweeping the figures off the board.

Lately, he has been showing an interest in poetry. Unfortunately, it is of a one-sided nature. He is willing to spend hours overhauling the classics to find a poor rhyme or wrong turn of phrase. Whenever he spots one his deafening guffaws cause the entire flat to reverberate.

His character is getting worse from day to day.

Only elementary decency restrains me from presenting him to someone else.

Then I wouldn't like to disappoint my mother-in-law. There is quite a bond of affection between her and Robby.

Vladislav Krapivin

MEETING MY BROTHER

EXPECT 'MAGELLAN'

I

THOSE who have visited Konsata will remember a steep narrow staircase leading to the shore. It starts at a little colonnaded landing and stops just short of the water-line, at a strip of ground, covered with porous stone and gravel that runs beneath the yellowish-white cliffs and extends from the South Valley to the Northern Spit where an obelisk – a monument to the lost astronauts – pierces the sky like a needle on a slant.

It is a good place for collecting brightly-coloured stones polished smooth by the waves, and hunting ill-humoured black crabs. Boys from the school to the south of Ratalsky Cosmodrome always halt there on their way home. Having crammed their pockets with treasures whose value is never appreciated by adults, they leap up the steep steps of the old staircase in preference to using the escalator twisting down the cliffs not a hundred yards away.

I had just finished writing my report of the third expedition to the Amazon basin. Now I had a whole month to read any books I fancied, a pleasure I had missed very much during the days of hard work.

With a book of poetry or some of Randin's short stories I would go to the top landing of the old staircase. It was a deserted place. Grass grew in cracks in the flagstones. Birds nested in the scrolls of heavy capitals.

For a few days I was alone there. Then a tall dark-complexioned man wearing a grey jacket of an unusual cut appeared. At first, as if by silent agreement, we ignored each other. But as we met frequently and hardly anybody else came there, we began to greet each other. I read my book and the stranger, apparently preoccupied and worried, seemed unwilling to enter into conversation.

The man usually came towards evening, when the sun was already low over the Northern Spit beyond which the white houses of Konsata were visible. The sea would be losing its blueness and the waves taking on a grey metallic tinge. In the east, caught in the reflected rays of the setting sun, the arches of the old launching pad turned pink. It stood at the edge of the Ratalsky Cosmodrome like a monument to times before interplanetary liners were adapted for vertical take-off.

When he got to the landing the stranger would settle down on the socle of a column, prop his chin on his hand and sit in silence.

He came to life when the schoolchildren appeared on the shore. Moving to the top step of the staircase he would watch their games, apparently waiting for one fair-haired boy in a black-and-orange striped jacket to notice him and run up. Whenever the boy ran fast his tiger-coloured jacket flapped like a gay banner.

A striking change would come over the stranger. Joyously he would greet the boy and, chattering animatedly, they would leave, nodding to me as they went.

At first I thought them father and son. But then one day I overheard the boy shouting to somebody as he ran:

'I'm going to meet my brother!'

From the brothers' talk I learned later that the elder one was called Alexandr.

It happened about a week after my first encounter with Alexandr. He came at his usual time, and sat down by the column, whistling some strange, harsh tune. I was reading inattentively because I knew Valentin Randin's *Song of the Blue Planet* almost by heart. From time to time I would glance at Alexandr and think that his face was somehow familiar.

It was a windy day. As I turned the pages of my tattered volume, one fluttered away. With a gentle rustle over the stones it settled at Alexandr's feet. He picked it up and rose to bring it to me. I got up too. We met in the middle of the landing.

It was the first time I had seen Alexandr so close. He was much younger than I thought. The lines at the bridge of his nose made his face look severe. But when he smiled, they disappeared.

'Not a very interesting book, I suppose?' he said, handing me the page.

'It's not that. You see, I've read it many times.'

I wanted our talk to continue, and added:

'Your brother is late today.'

'He said he'd be late, but it slipped my mind.'

Alexandr sat down beside me and asked to see the book. It was amazing that he did not know Randin's stories, but I did not comment. He opened the book holding the pages down with his hand on which I noticed an uneven scar.

Alexandr caught my look.

'That's an old one... I got it back at Yellow Rose.'

Now I knew.

'The Snezhnaya planet?' I exclaimed. 'You are Alexandr Sneg!'

It was recent history: the unusual broadcasts, the special issues of magazines with pictures of Alexandr and his three comrades. All over the Earth people repeated their names.

Before me was a man who had returned to the Earth three hundred years after leaving it. But it was not that alone that was so surprising. After all the *Banderilla* and *Musson* had also spent over two centuries in the cosmos. And though the story of the photon frigate which had carried Sneg back was more unusual than the others, it was not his case alone that puzzled me.

'Alexandr,' I said, thinking about the strange discrepancy, 'it took three hundred years, after all . . . And the boy is no more than twelve. How can he be your brother?'

'You are an archaeologist I know,' said Alexandr after a pause. 'You are more conscious of time than others. And you understand people ... Will you help me if I tell you everything?'

'I'll try.'

'Apart from myself, what I am going to tell you is known only to three other people. They can't help me. I want your advice. But where should I start? ... Well, everything began here on this very staircase.'

2

Everything started with the staircase.

It was the first time that Naal had been there since the death of his parents. The sea, bordered by the broad arc of the town's white buildings, was blue and glittering, with here and there the white crests of waves. It lay calm and sun-lit as though no ships had ever been claimed by its hidden depths.

Naal ran down the staircase gaining speed with each step. Soon gulping in the damp and salty wind, he was running as hard as he could to reach the enormous blue expanse.

He stumbled on a rough stone, twisted his ankle, and fell. His foot hurt but not unbearably. Biting his lip and limping he continued to go down. Like every boy Naal believed that salt water was the best medicine for cuts and abrasions. He took off his sandals and was about to go into the water when he spotted a big black crab. Involuntarily he jumped back.

To surrender to a momentary fear is one thing, to show the white feather is quite another. To test himself and to take revenge on the crab Naal resolved to catch the black hermit and fling it far into the sea, as far as he could.

Sensing danger the crab hurried away and hid among the stones.

'Now look out!' said the boy under his breath as he heaved a big flat stone. As it flopped into the water the crab tried to scramble away. But Naal had lost all interest in it: he had seen a small blue box, round and smooth as a sea-polished stone, lying on the wet sand. It was a mystery how it had got there.

The boy sat down on the sand and inspected it. It was firmly sealed. Naal spent over an hour scratching it with the buckle of his belt before he managed to pry it open. A strange badge wrapped in a sheet of old paper lay inside it – a golden branch with a tangle of stars in its leaves. On the stem was stamped a single word – 'Research.'

Naal examined the badge and quite forgot about the piece of paper. He would have ignored it altogether had not the wind thrown it into his lap. The boy smoothed it out – it was a page from an extremely old magazine. The box had been water-tight and the paper was unspoiled.

The boy started reading, making out the old lettering with great difficulty. His face grew very grave when, towards the end of the page, he found words as striking as the sudden loud twang of a tent string.

Two hours later some schoolchildren came and found Naal sitting in the same place with his elbows on a sun-warmed stone intently watching the white crests of the breaking waves.

'We've been looking for you everywhere,' said the eldest boy. 'We didn't know you had come back here. Why are you sitting alone?'

Naal did not hear. The wind blew sharper now, and the waves came pounding in. Have you ever heard the roaring of the waves? Above the sound of the surf is heard the boom as the waves crash and then the hiss of the waters as they spread over the shore ...

3

Like the other schoolchildren in South Valley, he delighted in flying high on the swing in dangerous proximity to twisted and gnarled old trees and chasing a bright-coloured ball among the trees of the sun-flooded grove. He was not very keen on learning the history of the discoveries of the bigger planet. He could run faster than many boys but his swimming was not above average. He was an eager participant in every game but never excelled at any of them. Only once did he manage to do what not everyone else could.

A springy branch whipped the golden badge with the blue stars off the front of his shirt and it fell into the water. He could see it sinking deeper and deeper. Without a second's hesitation he dived from a six-metre sheer cliff, by some miracle missing the sharp stones below.

Soon he was climbing back. One hand clutched the badge, and with the other he started in obstinate silence to wring the water out of his shirt.

No one knew where he had got the badge or why he valued it so much, but nobody asked him. After all, a boy may have his secrets. After his parents died Naal seemed to grow up all at once; he was often silent and ignored his friends' questions.

Outwardly his life went on very much the same. Even before, Naal used to spend the greater part of his time at school. Both his father and mother had been experts on probing the ocean depths and would often leave on expeditions. But now the boy knew that the bathyscaphe 'Reindeer' would never come back, never again would he see his father coming through the leafy avenue over there, a man he could run to meet, throw his arms round, and forget everything in the world.

Months passed. There were many quiet morning hours spent in study at school, there were days full of sunshine, noisy play and welcome rain. Perhaps the grief would have passed, had not one day the waves brought the small blue box, no one knew from where, and deposited it by the old staircase. No, the box was not a memento of the lost bathyscaphe.

At night when the orange reflections of the Ratalsky beacons fell on the window panes, he would take the crumpled page of the magazine out of the blue box. He did not need any light, he knew every line by heart. The magazine, published about three hundred years before, told of the launching of the photon space cruiser *Magellan.*

In his history book on flights to stars the cruiser was dealt with in one short dry passage: 'The *Magellan* was launched to one of the yellow stars with the aim of finding a planet resembling Earth. The crew obviously used incorrect information received from the cruiser *Globe* which was later presumed lost. The *Magellan* was expected to return in one hundred and twenty years. However, nothing was heard of it. It was presumed that its young inexperienced astronauts, misled by what must have been a legend, perished before they reached their goal.'

The book did not even give their names. Naal learned them from the page he had found. The captain's name was Alexandr Sneg.

Naal once heard from his father that one of his ancestors had been an astronaut. That day by the sea when he read the name Sneg he experienced both pride and bitter resentment. Resentment with his history book for the miserly and obviously incorrect passage about the cosmonauts. There could have been numerous reasons for the loss of the cruiser. Was the crew really to blame?

'Maybe they didn't find anything on that yellow star and continued to fly? What if they are still flying?' thought Naal arguing with the history book. But just as the thought struck him he shut his eyes tight as if frightened by the very idea. He saw very clearly the long dark avenue in the school garden, and at the other end of it – the tall man in the silvery jacket of an astronaut, the man Naal would run to greet, forgetting everything else in the world.

But what if he never came back? Why, he could still come back, time in cosmos ships passes only one-tenth as quickly as on the Earth. What if the cruiser were to come back? In that case Naal would meet not an ancestor or a stranger from another century, but his own brother. At the bottom of the page the boy had read what somebody had said to the crew of the *Magellan.*

'... Do not forget the old names. Many years hence you will come back and the grandsons of your friends will meet you as their own friends. The grandsons of your brothers will become your brothers ...'

Naal knew that these were only words. Nevertheless, he could clearly picture how it would happen. It would be morning ...

He could see that morning: the bright sun quite high in the sky, and the sky so blue that the white houses, the white clothes of the people and the silvery body of the spaceship had a blue tinge. The auxiliary rockets had gently lowered it on to the cosmodrome only a moment before. It stood perfectly still, supported by the black cylinders of the photon reflectors – a huge space cruiser, a shining tower with a black fin, a hundred and fifty metres long with the name *Magellan* printed in clear light-coloured old-fashioned lettering on it. Naal saw the tiny figures of the astronauts slowly descend the spiral staircase. Any moment now they would step onto the ground and walk towards the people. Naal, standing in front of the others, would be the first to meet them. He would ask right away which was Alexandr Sneg. Then ... No, he would say nothing. He would simply introduce himself – he too was Sneg ...

Naal was not accustomed to hiding his joys and sorrows.

Yet he didn't tell anybody about all this. Without realizing it he started dreaming about a miracle. But could one believe in miracles? Still, sometimes at night as he watched the reflections of the cosmodrome's beacons, Naal would take that crumpled page out. After all, everyone had a right to a dream even if that dream happened to be a futile one.

Miracles do not happen. But the same year, through a strange coincidence, the fifth pilot station received a call signal which rocked the whole planet: '*Magellan* calling Earth, *Magellan* calling Earth. Can you hear me? Expect my arrival. Over to you.'

4

The moon was not up yet though the upper part of the Power Ring could already be seen over the hills as a high irregular arc. Its yellowish diffused light seeped through the window to lie in a wide stripe across the carpet.

Naal switched off his wrist radio. There was no additional news. He could wait no longer. After a moment's hesitation he jumped up, hurriedly dressed and made his bed. Throwing his jacket over his shoulders he went to the window. It was slightly open. It could not be shut properly because outside grew a purple Martian convolvulus which clung with its tiny tendrils to the cornice outside. The thin stem would be cut off should the window be shut tight.

Outside the bushes glistened after the recent rain, and the white walls and the wide windows of the school had a barely perceptible greenish tinge. A ray of orange light appeared momentarily in the sparse clouds over the hills. The Ratalsky cosmodrome was again signalling somebody.

Naal opened the window and stepped out onto the path.

Alexei Oscar, the rector of the school, was not yet in bed. When the door opened, it let in fresh air that smelled of rain and stirred the pages of the book he was reading.

A boy stood at the door.

'Is that you, Naal?'

'Yes.'

For the first time Naal told his story; in a hurry to get it over, the words fairly tumbled out.

Oscar rose and turned to the window. Despite the general opinion he did not consider himself an experienced teacher. He simply possessed a knack of arriving at the right decision at the right time. But now he was at a loss. What could he say? Try to explain things to this boy, try to dissuade him from doing what he had decided to do? But would he be able to? Would he be right in doing so?

The rector remained silent for so long that it became embarrassing.

'Look here, Naal,' he started, and stopped, not knowing how to continue. 'It's late ...'

'Oscar, please let me go to the Shore of Summer,' said the boy softly. It was not even a request: his voice was full of anguish very much like that invincible yearning for the Earth which drives cosmonauts to desperate actions.

There are things that make the usual conceptions and rules powerless. What could Oscar say? Only that it was late and that Naal could go in the morning. But did it matter?

'I'll take you to the station,' said Oscar.

'No, don't bother. It's better if I go alone.'

And he left.

Oscar moved over to the videophone, called the Summer Shore, then dialled the call number of the pilot station, and pressed hard on the key of the emergency signal.

Nobody answered. The automatic service gave a soothing answer:

'All's well.'

THE NIGHT JOURNEY

I

It would have been much better if Naal had not taken that particular road.

He decided to take the path over the hills since it was shorter. In a quarter of an hour he was at the pass. Above the rounded hill tops hung the white moon in the pale ellipsis of Power Ring. On his right the Ratalsky beacons winked slowly. The lights of Konsata, partly obscured by a small range, gleamed on his left. Beyond the wide arc of lights, the sea was like a carpet gleaming dully in the moonlight.

The enormous black bulk of Ratalsky bridge – an old launching pad – cut across the whole width of the valley.

Up to now Naal had no hesitation and looked forward to the meeting. The news of the *Magellan* was so sudden and miraculous that his joy left no room for anxiety.

Anxiety appeared as soon as he saw the launching pad. He could not have explained why he suddenly felt that way. Could it be the very size and gloominess of those two-hundred-metre high arches rising before him like some gigantic gateway? They seemed to bring home to him the unfathomable magnitude of everything connected with the cosmos, the great distances travelled by the *Magellan*, and those three hundred years ... 'The grandchildren of your brothers will become your brothers!' But those were only words, and uttered three hundred years ago at that!

The black supports of the launching pad were like a double line of giants silently asking the boy where he was going, and why? What foolish thoughts was he harbouring in his head?

Naal looked around as if searching for reassurance. But the lights of the South Valley were obscured behind a hill.

He stopped for a moment, then darted towards the

launching pad. He ran in a direct line through the tall, still wet grass. Some prickly plant scratched his leg. He paused, pulled the plant out furiously, and began to run again. He ran hard to prevent that strange anxiety from catching up with him. Having crossed that wide strip of meadow, the black gates of the Ratalsky bridge would be left behind...

2

The express carriage of the ring-way train which ran from the Summer Shore to the northern tip of the continent was empty. Naal settled in an armchair with his feet tucked under him, and watched the darkness beyond the windows fly back at a speed of five hundred kilometres per hour.

He was tired. Any other time he would certainly have fallen asleep but now the same old anxiety plagued him like a tiresome bass string: 'What if he said nothing in reply? Or took it all as a joke? And would a cosmos hero returning to Earth after three hundred years have any time to spare for a mere boy?'

Suddenly he pictured the huge cosmodrome full of thousands of people. Thousands of greetings, thousands of hands stretched out for a handshake. What would he be doing there? And what could he say?

He was struck by the thought that instead of spending the night in the town, of waiting for the morning and the landing of the ship, he would tell Alexandr everything right now.

'Pilot-5' station had been in constant touch with the cruiser. The station was some forty kilometres from the Summer Shore. That meant another five minutes.

At the next turning Naal stepped off onto a moving ring-platform. Jumping from one concentric platform to another at a slower speed he reached the motionless centre, and went out through a tunnel.

Before him was a black expanse. Behind – the soft lights of the platform, far ahead the spire of the pilot station glowed blue. The wind rustled in the grass, and that sound somehow reassured him. He set off towards the blue spire.

Here, too, were signs of recent rain. Damp leaves clung to his knees, and the wind's breath was warm and damp.

Soon Naal reached the road where the going was easier; the wind blew stronger, trying to whip his light jacket off his shoulders.

3

For some time 'Pilot-5' station had refused to divulge any information. All inquiries were met by the automatic answer: 'Everything is going well.' Many people tried to tune in on the cruiser's wave-length but failed because nobody knew the three-hundred-year-old systems.

The Jupiter intermediate station was the first to receive the news of the photon spaceship. Now the Earth was in direct communication with it, and the pilots did not leave the station for a moment: three of them were on duty by the vectorial beacon, while the fourth slept in an armchair. The ship's crew had already passed the cruiser's control over to the scientists on the ground. The pilots expected to land the spaceship on the Shore cosmodrome.

Only a few hours previously Sergei Koster had established two-way communications with the spaceship. But so far the crew had given no more detailed news than the reading of the automatic systems necessary for their landing.

The pilots manoeuvred the ship to a circular orbit, where it became an Earth satellite with the same orbital speed. Sergei was at the end of the transmitting co-ordinates when Miguel Nuvios said:

'Somebody has been signalling for over an hour with an inquiry.'

'Somebody's having a bout of sleeplessness,' said Sergei

without turning around. He was closely watching the vector crossing through the cosmodrome – a black spot on a luminous map.

'Six signals – an urgent call. I don't think it's the usual curiosity.'

'If it was something important it would come in direct.'

'Well, I don't know ...'

A few minutes later Sergei, too, heard the sound of an urgent call. But neither he nor the two other pilots at their posts by the auxiliary transmitters could spare time to answer the videophone.

'Miguel, take the call, can't you?' asked Sergei.

But Miguel was fast asleep in his armchair.

The signal was not repeated.

Another thirty minutes passed. The spaceship's automatic systems received the final order. Sergei closed his eyes in relief. But the red-coloured figures continued to dance before his aching eyes.

At that moment somebody tugged at his sleeve. The pilot took his hand away from his eyes and saw a boy of about twelve, fair and suntanned, his unbuttoned striped jacket revealing a golden badge on a light green shirt, his legs covered with fresh scratches.

The boy was looking up at Sergei. In his hurry to explain everything at once he spoke so confusedly that the pilot could hardly understand him.

'What are you talking about? How did you get here?' he asked.

Reaching the central building Naal went through a door and found himself in a long narrow corridor. His step echoed as he went along the smooth shining floor on which the big lamps were reflected as though it were a sheet of glass. Once again Naal heard those nagging anxious sounds in his head. He felt uneasy, a hard lump was in his throat and his heart beat madly like a ball bumping down stairs.

The corridor ended in a sharp turn. Naal walked up a wide

flight of steps; hesitating for a moment with his hand raised, he screwed up his courage and pushed the frosted glass door open. He found himself in a round hall with low walls and a transparent cupola sectioned off with strange white lines through which stars peeped. The black-and-white checkerboard sloped gently upwards towards a small platform in the centre, where three men stood beside a black conical apparatus. In one of the chairs round the platform slept a fourth man. The men by the apparatus were talking, and their voices echoed and sounded unnatural. Every word reached Naal yet failed to make sense. His head was spinning, perhaps from tiredness. Everything seemed unreal. He walked across the black-and-white floor, stepped up onto the platform and tugged at the sleeve of one of the men. The man turned. His look of surprise told Naal that his approach had not been observed.

Coming straight to the point, he said:

'I am here to meet my brother ...'

Everything had a dreamlike quality. As he talked, Naal could hear his own voice bounce off the walls and disappear in the enormous hall. He could not remember how long he had been talking. Perhaps a very short time. Signals flashed on and off on the control panels along the circular walls, blue flashes swiftly changing their pattern.

'Tell me please, pilot, he won't refuse, he'll answer me?' Naal pleaded, overcoming his torpor for a moment. There was a short, tense silence. Then somebody said something which, in its simplicity and ordinariness, was in strong contrast with the dramatic discussion that was taking place.

'So that's how it is ...'

Somebody else called to the sleeping man:

'Miguel, Miguel, listen to this!'

Lights still darted across the panels, and the senior pilot, Sergei, suddenly remarked:

'You are asleep, my boy.'

He picked him up and put him into a big soft chair. But Naal was not asleep. He kept his eys on the dancing light signals and heard the words droning under the cupola:

'The man ...'

'The three centuries ...'

'Wasn't frightened ... But what if ...?'

'He's asleep.'

'No, he isn't.'

The voice which said 'he isn't' asked:

'What's your name, brother of the cosmonaut?'

'Naal.'

Though the question was not asked again he felt that they did not understand him, so he said:

'Nathanial Sneg.'

'Sneg ...' the voice repeated.

'A strange combination ...'

'Nothing strange about it,' Naal wanted to say. 'They called me that in honour of Nathaniel Leed, the Captain of the Bathyscaphe "Svet" ...'

Somebody touched the chair, and said:

'Asleep ...'

'I'm not,' said Naal, and opened his eyes. 'Did the *Magellan* answer, pilot?'

Sergei bent over him:

'Now you go to sleep ... They said they'll meet you in a week's time. The crew decided to land in the forest zone ... Evidently they want to avoid a noisy reception. They've been missing the feel of the ground, the wind, the forest. It'll take them a few days to reach the Summer Shore on foot as they plan.'

Naal's sleep quickly melted away.

'What about me? And the people? Don't they want to see them?'

'Now, don't take on so,' said Sergei. 'They promised to meet you in a week.'

Now Naal could see that the hall at the pilot station was

not particularly big. The sky above the transparent cupola was low and overcast.

'Where are they going to land?' he asked.

'They asked us not to tell anybody.'

'Not even me?'

'Well ... at the White Cape Peninsula.'

Naal got to his feet.

'Stay the night here,' suggested Sergei. 'And then we'll see.'

'No, I think I'll be getting on home.'

'I'll see you off.'

'Don't bother.'

So that was that. There was once a silly fairytale which, like a fool, he had believed. Well, three hundred years ...

Without listening to what the pilot was saying he started off over the black-and-white checks, broke into a run, along the glassy floor in the corridor, along the gravel path outside. He was out in the black field again, headed for the distant platform. Now he walked slowly. He had nowhere to hurry to anymore. 'We'll meet in a week's time ...' If a person were looking forward to a meeting he would not wait one single hour.

4

Perhaps everything would have ended there. But a hundred paces before the station Naal came across the 'bee' park. A thought crossed his mind which at first seemed childish but ten steps later made him pause in his tracks. 'What if it were too late for Alexandr to change their plans when he heard the pilot tell him everything? After all, he is not alone,' thought Naal.

Hesitantly he approached the flying machines, feeling his heart beat fast with renewed hope. He was three months short of the earliest age – twelve – when a boy was allowed to pilot one of these 'bees'. Should he do right to break the rules?

Still undecided he climbed into the cabin and lowered the protective cowl. Then he checked the engine. Yellow lights twinkled encouragingly from the control board. He took off, lifting the 'cab' on its horizontal screws, opened the throttle, and headed North-east.

The high speed would enable him to reach the White Cape in two hours.

He must have slept part of the way for the flight seemed to have taken hardly any time at all. One thought was uppermost in his mind: 'I'll simply walk over and explain who I am. The rest doesn't matter now ...'

If they met him with an indifferent look he would go straight back to the cabin without another word, and fly back to the South-east.

The trouble came just when the 'bee' having passed a peaceful gulf mirroring the stars, was flying over a black mass of forest towards the promontory. The sky in the East was beginning to show blue while directly above him it was still dark. Somewhere up there hung the *Magellan* deserted by its crew.

In vain did Naal strain his eys searching for lights or at least the dark shape of the landing rocket. Twice he flew to the very tip of the promontory and back over the very tops of the trees. It was then that he felt the motor was turning more slowly. The storage batteries were spent. He realized he must have taken one of the machines that had not been serviced. He climbed as high as possible to have a good look over the mass of forest. He rose until the motor gave out, the screws stopped turning, and his 'bee' let out its wings and started gliding slowly to Earth.

When it was too late Naal realized he had made a mistake. Underneath as far as the eye could see was forest, and a normal landing was out of the question.

Somehow the thought did not frighten him. Watching the tree tops rushing back beneath him he tried to keep his machine straight. Next moment he was in among the tree tops, automatically he applied the brakes. There was a crash and a series of sharp jolts. He felt himself flung from his seat, something pressing against his shoulder, and dry aromatic twigs clinging to his cheek. 'I wonder where the rocket is?' he thought as he stretched himself out on the grass.

THE FOURTH SUN

I

'Naturally, neither the pilots nor the boy knew the reasons for our strange decision,' said Alexandr. 'It was our utter confusion. Not just the understandable confusion which an unexpected piece of news can cause but a real helplessness and fear. What answer could we give?

'I won't speak about the flight itself. All flights are similar unless they end in disaster – work, long anabiotic sleep ... It took us twelve years – fifty for you on Earth – to reach the planet of our destination. We by-passed the Yellow Rose.

'At first we tasted the bitterness of a scientific experiment that failed. Before us was an ice-locked land, devoid of any life, without the murmur of forests, or the lapping of waves. A big bright yellow sun wrapped in a haze of cold mist hung suspended over a broken range of mountains. It really resembled a yellow rose. The frozen ocean glistened pink and yellow. Deep blue vapours collected in the crevices between the rocks, cracks in the ice and the shadows of gloomy precipices. Ice ... Cold glittering ... Still.

'The only thing that was a pleasant surprise was the air. Real, very like that surrounding the Earth, and as cold as the water from a mountain stream. On the very first day we abandoned our helmets, and breathed the air through clenched teeth because of the cold. We were terribly tired of the chemically pure "unleavened" insipid air of the ship's compartments. To my mind it was the air that caused that fomenting longing to be back on Earth. Even to think about it is horrible. But there, on the Snezhnaya planet, we stopped feeling it so acutely. There was something familiar in that ice-bound bewitched world. But the realization did not come to us right away. Every time we left the cruiser we saw that kingdom of snow, stone and ice ...'

2

A blue mist which turned the orange sunbeams green where they shone down through the spaces between the sheer walls filled the deep gorges. There they sparkled from the broken ice like milliards of emeralds. When the sun's rays reached the bottom they reflected from the ice crystals great bouquets of fantastic lights.

The night sky patterned with the outlines of blue constellations was like a black wall around the *Magellan*. From time to time the high transparent clouds would become a shimmering yellow and light would stream down the ice-bound mountain slopes illuminating, here and there, huge piles of rocks.

Nevertheless, that cold planet was living. At times the heavy clouds would creep from the west obscuring the orange-coloured setting sun and wiping the ugly black shadows off the ice fields. They would bring snow, real snow, just as if it were somewhere by the Kara Sea or in the Antarctic. It melted in one's hands turning into ordinary water. Then the water became warm.

One day the men found a valley free of ice and snow in the southern hemisphere. There were bare cliffs, stones that shone silver in the water, and course sand on the banks of a sparkling stream that cascaded down the rocks. In the spray numerous, tiny rainbows seemed to be trying to bring the world out of its frozen slumber.

A short distance from the waterfall Karr found a small

black-leafed plant clinging to a rock. He took off his glove and was on the point of pulling out the thin knotty stem when the plant's black pointed leaves moved to meet his hand. Instinctively Karr pulled back.

'Leave it alone,' was the prudent advice of Larsen. 'Who knows ...'

But Karr took the advice in his own way. Smiling he moved his hand over the black plant, and as before the small narrow leaves stretched towards it.

'It's after warmth,' he said softly. Then he called the expedition's biologist who had dropped behind. 'Tael, here at last is a real discovery for you!'

But the navigation officer failed to grasp its full significance at the time.

That evening all five men gathered in the mess of the Magellan: Knud Larsen, blond and broad-shouldered, good-humoured and absent-minded in everything that was not related to his computers; the two Africans, high-spirited little biologist Tael, and the navigator Tey Karat known usually as Karr; Georgi Rogov, the pilot and astronomer, fair-haired like Larsen, but almost as dark-skinned as the Africans, and the youngest of the crew. And, finally, Alexandr Sneg who was their senior reconnaissance navigator and an artist. He had been so busy with his sketches of late that he had passed most of his duties over to Karr.

When they were all gathered in the mess Karr said:

'This is a strange planet, don't you agree? But one thing is clear: it it wasn't for the sheet of ice there would be life here. It is evident too that the sun, that is the Yellow Rose, will melt the ice sometime. But who can say how many millenniums it will take? Shouldn't we melt the ice ourselves?'

He suggested firing four artificial suns over the Snezhnaya planet according to the system of Academician Vorontsov. The system was a well-tried and simple one. Such atomic suns were fired as long ago as in the first decades after the destruction of all arms and people were able at last to divert nuclear energy to peaceful purposes. About the same time, the ice in Greenland and the coastal regions of the Antarctic continent was melted.

'But why four?' asked Georgi.

'That's the minimum. We can't have fewer ... wouldn't be enough to melt all the ice, and the eternal winter would grip the planet again.'

However the four suns would consume two thirds of the remaining ezan, the cosmic fuel. That meant that the ship would not have enough left to generate the required speed. It would take two hundred and fifty years to reach the Earth. Most of the flight would have to be spent in a state of anabiotic sleep. Two hundred and fifty years ... But that would enable them to bring yet another planet within the reach of the people – a new outpost of humanity in the cosmos. The long flight would not have been in vain.

'What is needed, then?' asked Larsen.

'For us to agree,' Karr looked at each in turn.

'I'm for,' said Larsen.

'Same here,' exclaimed Tael.

Georgi inclined his head in silence.

'I'm against!' said Sneg firmly, and stood up.

A few seconds of silent surprise followed, then Sneg started speaking.

He said that it was silly to turn the planet into an incubator. That people should not be afraid of severe ice or of fighting against the nature of a strange planet. That without fighting life would lose its meaning ... What if their artificial suns suddenly died out before all the ice melted? What would become of the first dwellers on the Snezhnaya planet if permanent winter returned? But even if the suns did not die out and the ice was melted what would the people see? Bare mountains, valleys without vegetation, grey desert ...

They listened, and there was a moment when each was

ready to agree with him. Not only because his words seemed to be convincing – his very passion and persistence were convincing. Sneg always argued that way when he felt strongly he was in the right. It was with the same heat that he had defended the right to fly to 'his own' star.

3

His friends remembered him in the big room of the Stella Palace standing before a pale thin man and saying with a fierce directness:

'I am surprised that the Union of Astronauts should entrust the decision of a question like this to you alone – a man who has no ability to believe in legends!'

The man grew pale, but the only sign of his exasperation was a slight confusion in his quiet answer:

'Every youth who has gone beyond the orbit of Jupiter considers himself well prepared for freedom in cosmic research and is ready to fly even to the centre of the Galaxy. It's ridiculous. All these fairy tales about the planets of the Yellow Rose have turned your head. The Yellow Rose is an insidious star. It's all very alluring, naturally; it's certainly true ... fairy tales always attract.'

'You claim a knowledge of eternal truths but you forget one of them: every legend contains a grain of truth. We believe there are planets ...'

Rotais inclined his head.

'I allow myself the right to end this pointless talk. I don't see that you have any claim to undertake an expedition of free research ... May I add that I feel distressed and find it difficult to speak: an hour ago Valentin Yantar had an accident and I am in a hurry to see him.'

Obviously he was not in a great hurry because when Alexandr came to the house of the old cosmonaut, the only people he met there were the doctors. He learned that Yantar had refused to have an operation.

'Flying is not for me any more ... As to living, well, I've lived long enough.'

Silently Sneg entered the room where the astronaut was lying. Yantar said to the perplexed doctor:

'Please leave us alone.'

The room was in semi-darkness. Though the windows were curtainless, branches of the flowering apple trees pressed close against them. Alexandr stood by the bed. Yantar was covered with a white blanket pulled up to his chin. On it lay his long matted blond beard and on his lined forehead was a streak of blood.

'Nobody can understand me except you,' Alexandr began. 'Others might accuse me of heartlessness, of being egoistic ... But you and I, we can be frank with each other. You'll never be able to fly any more.'

'True ...'

'They won't allow my team to do our own research,' said Alexandr quietly. 'Would you pass to us your right to make a second flight? We'll go.'

'You mean, to Leda? To my planet?' Neither his hands nor his head moved, but his eyes sparkled with joy. 'You've decided?'

At this moment Yantar must have seen the blue world of Leda, the planet whose secret had never been fully revealed, the ruins of its turquoise towns, and its white mountains rising over violet masses of impenetrable forests forever shrouded in poisonous bluish mist. But the strange vision disappeared, and again he saw before him the stern, tense face of Alexandr.

'No, I shouldn't say "mine",' said Yantar in a hollow tone.

'Every one of us has his own star,' said Sneg.

He sat down by the bed and gave a detailed account of everything: the latest news from the *Globe* about the mystery of the Yellow Rose, the plan for free research worked out by the five astronauts, his recent talk with Rotais.

'The Leda needs archaeologists. We are reconnaissance scouts. We want to find a planet with air like we have here. People need such planets.'

Yantar closed his eyes.

'Good... You have my right.'

'He won't believe me,' argued Alexandr recalling the impassive pale face of Rotais.

'Then take my badge. It's in the blue shell on the table.'

In a shell brought from the Leda lay a golden badge with blue stars and an inscription 'Research'.

Alexandr looked at the badge, then at the wounded astronaut. For the first time in those few last days his resolution failed him. He clenched his teeth and withdrew his hand.

'It's yours,' repeated Yantar. 'It's yours right now.'

'Break that window,' he commanded Alexandr when he took the badge. 'No, don't open it, break it ... It's old and will yield easily ... Good,' he said, when he hear the tinkle of the broken glass.

Alexandr also broke a sizable bough off a tree, letting the sun into the room.

'Happy voyage!' said Valentin Yantar, forcing down the growing pain with an effort. 'May all of you return back to Earth!'

'That doesn't happen too often!'

'The more reason to wish it...'

As Sneg was going out he met Rotais and showed him the badge in the open palm of his hand. Rotais shrugged his shoulders and inclined his head, indicating a hidden resentment with the young astronaut's action and at the same time a forced acquiescence. No one could deny a cosmonaut the right to a second flight – that is a cosmonaut was entitled to a second expedition any time, on any of the ships ready to start, after discovering a new planet and safely returning to earth. He could also pass that right on to another Captain.

For a second Alexandr could see again the face of Yantar,

the famous Captain of the *Research*, his wrinkled forehead with the bloody scar, and his blue eyes which seemed to reflect the fantastic world of Leda. 'You mean to Leda? To my planet?' Nevertheless, the old astronaut understood Alexandr. But Rotais?

Alexandr turned round and coldly said to Rotais, whose back was turned to him:

'Kindly inform the eastern cosmodrome that we've chosen the *Magellan*!'

He had done more than anybody else to make this flight possible. And it was more difficult for him to leave than it was for the others. Each of them had relatives, of course, but he alone was also leaving his sweetheart behind.

Their tacit friendship seemed strange to outsiders. Not often were they seen together. They seldom spoke of one another. Only their close friends knew of their love.

A week before the start Alexandr met her in a new, sunny garden, the place which today is known as Konsata's Golden Park. The wind was tearing at the leaves, and the sun danced on the white sand on the path. The girl was silent.

'But you knew that I was an astronaut,' said Sneg.

He could be quite calm when necessary.

Just before the start he handed her the badge...

One day looking by chance into their *Magellan* mess-room Georgi saw Sneg take out a small stereo-photograph and place it in front of him, then look at it intently in silence.

'I would hide this picture forever, if I were you,' said Georgi.

Alexandr looked up at him with a mixture of mockery and surprise.

'And that would make me forget, you think?'

He put his hand over his eyes, then with a few rough strokes of his pencil on a piece of cardboard he drew the girl's face, a remarkably true likeness.

'There you are.'

It was their eighth year of flight in the *Magellan*, according to the ship's own time.

4

Yet it was Alexander Sneg, once so eager to start on this expedition, who was now defending the ice-locked planet, as if they suggested its doom rather than its resurrection.

'A grey desert, sickly little plants! Even if there is not any ice, what will there be? A dead land, dead stones.'

'People'll create everything!' argued Tael. 'Everything they need.'

'But let me add this,' continued Sneg. 'We can't rob people of the world we found here. It is beautiful, this world. Don't you understand that? Don't you see it?'

He threw his sketches down on the table. With bated breath they looked again at what they had seen before but which they had forgotten, depressed by this kingdom of ice. Sneg found remarkably true colours; orange-black sunsets, blue ravines full of glowing mist, mornings which fired golden sparks off the ice, the yellow sky with its untidy heaps of clouds ...

The pages rustled as they were turned over. At last Karr said:

'All right. But who would want it – cold and death for the sake of beauty? What's the use of this dead ice?'

'It's not dead,' Alexandr shook his head. 'There is its own life here, the wind, the streams, the bushes ... Everything here is coming slowly to life. We shouldn't hurry it, or we'll have a desert here.'

'It won't be a desert. There'll be an ocean, blue and boundless, like the oceans on Earth. The melted ice'll give enough water. Waterfalls will roar here. Just think, Alexandr: thousands of silver waterfalls amidst the rocks and the rainbow-coloured mist. The severe nature will remain with a beauty all its own. There will be life, too. That's the kind of planet we set out to find.'

'There'll be an ocean, and islands overgrown with forests,' said Tael dreamily.

'Forests? You mean those black little bushes will grow into forests?'

'People will plant the forests!'

'On stones?'

'You're wrong, Alex,' Georgi, who had been silent up to now, said gently. 'Think of the Antarctic.'

Sneg was on the point of saying something when he sat down, suddenly tired, and said:

'All right, I give up.'

'And you'll take part in the necessary calculations?'

'In work, yes, but not in calculations. What sort of a mathematician do you think I am?'

5

They had been working for a long time, both with the help of their automatic machinery and pneumatic wrenches. Then they launched the four rockets into their orbits surrounded by a network of magnetic regulators. The rockets were not equipped with automatic pilots. Karr and Larsen piloted the two they had built, and later left them and parachuted down, safe in their special suits. They repeated the operation twice. The four rockets working on the cosmic fuel *RY*-202-ezan became the apices of a triangular pyramid, inside which the Snezhnaya planet seemed to be suspended.

They did not refer to the argument any more. Alexandr worked with enthusiasm. He even did the calculations for one of the artificial suns. Each had his own sun except Karr who undertook the general calculations and control.

When the last day of work was over, the crew of the *Magellan* gathered in the ravine which they had chosen for the control station.

'Well, spring-created gods,' said Karr with unnecessary solemnity.

'Everything's ready now,' Tael heaved a deep sigh.

'Ready?'

'Ready.'

The signal was given, and the three screens flashed dazzlingly. Mountains and piles of ice appeared on them illuminated apparently by two or three suns. The fourth screen remained blank.

'It's mine,' said Sneg.

The fourth sun remained unfired.

Nobody quite knew what had happened. Apparently the system of magnetic regulators was at fault. The smallest impetus, a jolt from an infinitesimal meteorite would be enough, perhaps, to start the sun off in a few seconds. But what were the chances of a meteorite hitting the rocket?

'Where's the harm? All right, it'll leave an ice cap like we had in the Antarctic once ... What the hell! Just think of it: a snowbound plateau named after Sneg!' exclaimed simple-hearted Larsen.

'Yes, marvellous,' said Alexandr dryly.

Then followed an awkward silence. None of them, naturally, thought that Sneg had calculated incorrectly on purpose. Alexandr himself understood this too, yet the fact remained that it was he who had failed!

'I'll take a rocket and break the regulators with my jet,' said Sneg quietly but firmly, after they all returned to the *Magellan*.

'Let's all turn in,' suggested Karr.

'Larsen, you check me,' called Sneg. 'I'll prove that it's possible.'

'You mean, to go to bed?'

'To break the holding back regulators and to escape the flare-up.'

Larsen obediently sat down by the keyboard of the electronic brain. Alexandr started dictating figures.

'As you see, it's possible in principle,' he said when the calculations were finished.

'In principle ...' growled Larsen. 'Don't be a fool, you'll burn.'

'No, Alex, let's go to bed,' said Georgi. 'Things aren't as bad as you think.'

But all of them knew that things were bad, very bad.

Two-thirds of the ezan had been used. It would take two hundred and fifty years to get back to Earth and they would return empty-handed. By that time the Snezhnaya planet would again be held in a grip of ice. Who knew when other people would come here again, and when they would fire the atomic suns? Yet they had seen to everything, almost. If there were no unforeseen errors the crew of the *Magellan* would bring to Earth the news of a planet ready for normal habitation. People needed such planets, outposts of humanity in the boundless universe, stepping-stones for further, longer strides.

They were awakened in the middle of the night by a shrill call signal. Alexandr's amplified voice said:

'I am in the rocket. Don't be cross with me, boys, but I have to try.'

'Alex, please,' said Georgi. 'We all ask you, don't. To hell with this planet. Think of the Earth.'

'I'll be all right.'

'You'll burn.'

'No, I won't.'

'Sneg, return immediately, it's an order!' shouted Karr.

'Now, Karr, please don't be angry ... But I'm the Captain.'

'Look, but you yourself wanted the planet to stay locked in ice,' pleaded Larsen.

They heard Alexandr's chuckle.

'Karr's to blame. He was so eloquent about the ocean, waterfalls, islands. And I'm an artist and wanted to paint it all.'

Karr cursed quietly.

'Switch your videophone on,' asked Tael.

Sneg obeyed and they saw his face on the screen. He was bending over the control board, whistling.

'Take care of yourself,' said Georgi.

Sneg nodded, still whistling.

'Just when we're supposed to return to Earth! Why are you doing it?' said Karr desperately. 'What if it flares up suddenly?'

'Well, you know yourself ... It has to be seen through ... to the end.'

The roar of the engine made further speech impossible. The image on the screen swayed, Alexandr's face became distorted through overloading. Then the overloading disappeared, and the speed began to slow down. High speed would have prevented Alexandr from making the necessary turn to hit the regulators with his jet. In silence they watched Alexandr's tense face – all that they could see. It continued until a blinding white flame flooded the screen ...

6

'How did you manage to escape?' I asked Alexandr.

He glanced at me from under his heavy brows.

'That's the whole point ... I'm Georgi Rogov. Sneg was killed ... D'you understand what we felt when the pilot told us about the boy? A boy on the Earth was waiting desperately for his brother. It's difficult for you to understand, perhaps. But for us who've been missing our Earth and the people for so many years, to us that longing and anxiety were feelings we knew well. It's especially difficult when you know that there won't be a single familiar face among those you see. Three hundred years ... Even their names would be forgotten. And suddenly a brother ... We understood the boy well, his longing for somebody to call his own. And then, too, it was very difficult to tell the truth. Impossible.

'It was Tael who found a solution. He gave the station an evasive answer which allowed us some time.

'"But that's not a way out," said Larsen. "What are we going to tell him later?"'

'"What's the boy's name?"' I asked.

'Karr told me, looking at me speculatively. But he didn't add anything.

'The engine of our landing rocket failed when we were quite close to Earth, so we parachuted to safety in our protective cosmic suits.

'It was still dark. The East was just beginning to turn blue. I don't remember everything. There was the smell of leaves and the damp earth. Tael stood with his dark face pressed against the trunk of a birch tree – just a blur of white in the dusk. Larsen threw himself down on the ground, exclaiming, "Just look at it, the grass..."

'My eyes were on the heavens. A bright yellow streak heralded the new day, while the sky above turned clear blue. It seemed to be ringing. I never knew that it could ring like a million singing strings. A light cloud directly overhead was slowly becoming filled with a fiery pink . . . Suddenly horror seized me. I seemed to be having the same poignant dream about the Earth which had tormented us on the Snezhnaya. My fear was like an electric shock. I lay down on the grass, and shut my eyes. I clung for all I was worth to the root of a bush. It was rough to the touch and wet...

'A moment later I released my grip and opened my eyes. The blue sky was ringing over the forest. Through the ringing I heard Larsen say again: "Just look at it, leaves..."

'Then the sun rose.

'Have you ever seen the sun rising from the ground? You must watch it lying down. The grass looks like some fantastic jungle from which the bright sun rises, turning the dewdrops into multi-coloured sparks.'

Naal was watching the sun through the grass. He remembered everything, and from the corner of his eye could even see the broken 'bee.' He felt neither excitement nor belated fear. Everything that happened during the previous night came to him as a muddled blur. The boy felt the futility of his cherished dream.

When the sun rose so that its lower edge touched the heads of the tall flowers growing by the edge of the little glade, Naal stood up. His head felt dizzy, and his hurt shoulder ached. He had been lucky after all, for the shock-absorbers set him down in the soft grass. He had fallen asleep where he was, so great was his weariness.

Slowly he looked around. He had nowhere to hurry to. All around him, for a hundred kilometres, was forest. The wind stirred the leaves.

At this moment somebody behind him exclaimed in happy surprise:

'Look – a boy.'

Naal turned round, and stood stock-still. He saw the men in blue flying suits covered with a criss-cross of broad white straps.

Feeling his heart stop, the boy shouted:

'You are from the *Magellan*!'

'Naal . . .' said the dark-complexioned fair-haired pilot.

'I was the last to notice him,' said Georgi, 'and the strange thing was that I had the impression that I knew the boy. Could it have been that I recalled myself as I was in my childhood? He stood tense, his whole body longing to rush to us. Small and fair, a dry blade of grass still sticking to his cheek, his shirt torn at the shoulder, and one of his knees scratched ... His eyes were on my face – very blue, wide-open eyes. I think I called him by name.

'At this moment Karr gave me a slight push on the shoulder, saying loudly: "Go and meet your brother Alexandr."

'You may say I acted selfishly,' continued Georgi. 'But at

that moment I didn't think that Naal wasn't my brother. If you knew what it is to meet a near one on this Earth when you never expected it ... But now I am beginning to think that perhaps I had no right to do so?'

I did not understand what he meant. Georgi explained:

'Alexandr fired the sun. The last one needed to melt the ice. There is an ocean and islands there now ... Had I the right to rob the boy of a brother like that?'

'A dead brother.'

'Yes, even a dead brother.'

'Well, Georgi,' said I, 'I can't judge. Perhaps Alexandr had another reason for risking his life? Are you sure he wanted to come back? His girl ...'

Georgi smiled shortly. Obviously he thought my question silly.

'Of course he did. He loved the Earth. Who doesn't want to go back to Earth?'

A silence fell.

'It can't go on like this,' he started again. 'I not only robbed the boy of his brother, I robbed Alexandr of his heroism. People should know the story of the fourth sun.'

'You also robbed yourself of your name. Georgi Rogov is supposed to have perished.'

'My name has no special value.'

'You've asked my advice, then here it is. Let everything remain as it is. The fourth sun won't grow dim because of it. You must think of Naal.'

'It's about him that I think all the time ... But what about Sneg?'

'The time will come when the people'll learn everything.'

'But the memory of Alexandr? The memory of his heroism? What he did is an example for the living to follow. Perhaps some day Naal will fire his own sun.'

I looked at Georgi. He was waiting for my objections. He wanted to hear them – they were restoring a brother to him I said:

'Perhaps ... True ... But over what planet will he fire his sun? Give him your knowledge, teach him, you are his brother. And he will make his sun shine.'

The sunset was gone without a trace. The half moon girdled on one side by the arc of the Power Ring hung low over the sea.

Running footsteps on the stone staircase cut our conversation short. Anyhow, there was nothing more to say.

They left, nodding to me as they went. The astronaut's hand held his little brother's firmly.

On the notebook open before me lies a golden badge whose story remained unknown. Naal gave it to me just before our take-off ...

We, a group of archaeologists, all flying to Leda, the planet whose secret Valentin Yantar failed to reveal. We are not expected back for a long time.

Perhaps eighty years hence among the many greeting us there will be one – small or big, it does not matter – as yet unknown boy, who will say to his friends: 'I've come to meet my brother!'

Sever Gansovsky

CHAIRMAN OF THE COMMISSION: *'You can read in several languages, are acquainted with higher mathematics, and can carry out certain kinds of work. Do you consider this makes a man of you?'*
OTARK: *'Certainly. Are people capable of anything else?'*
(STATE COMMISSION *material – From cross-examination of an* OTARK.)

A DAY OF WRATH

TWO men on horseback rode out of the valley, which was thickly overgrown with grass, and began to ascend the mountainside. In front, the forester sat astride a hook-nosed roan, Donald Betly, on a chestnut mare, brought up the rear. The mare stumbled on the stony mountain path and fell to its knees. Betly, who had been lost in thought, nearly flew out of the saddle, which was of English make with one belly-strap, and slipped down onto the horse's neck.

The forester waited for him higher up on the path.

'Keep its head up, it always stumbles,' he called out.

Betly bit his lip and glared at him in vexation. 'Damn him, he could have warned me,' he thought. He was mad at himself too because the mare had fooled him. She had inflated her belly when he saddled her so that strap would be loose.

He yanked on the reins so hard that the horse danced around and stepped back.

The path had levelled out again. They were travelling along a plateau. The tops of fir-wooded hills sloped ahead of them in the distance.

The horses were moving at a long-paced trot. Sometimes they would break into a brisk canter, racing each other. When the mare managed to get in front, Betly could see the thin, suntanned, clean-shaven cheeks of the forester, and his sombre-looking eyes, which seemed glued to the road, as if he were utterly unaware of his companion's presence.

'I'm too artless,' Betly thought to himself. 'And it never does me any good. I've spoken to him five times and all he does is grunt in answer, or pays no attention whatsoever. He doesn't give a damn about me. He seems to think that if a person likes to talk he's an empty-headed chatter-box who doesn't deserve respect. Out here in the sticks they don't know how to gauge things. A journalist doesn't mean a thing to them. Even journalists like ... Aw heck, I won't talk to him either, as far as that goes. What do I care . . .!'

Gradually his mood changed for the better. Betly was a man whom luck had always favoured and he considered that other people should enjoy life with the fervour that he did. He found the forester's reticence rather surprising, but he felt no enmity towards the man.

The weather had been bad from early morning, but the sky was beginning to clear up, and the fog had thinned. The greyish film in the sky had dispersed into separate clouds. Huge shadows swiftly sped over the darkened forests and ravines, accentuating the severe, wild, untrammelled character of the locality.

Betly clapped the mare on its damp, sweat-smelling neck.

'Your front feet must have been hobbled when you were let out to graze at nights, that's why you stumble. But it's all right, we'll get along.'

He let out the reins and caught up with the forester.

'I say, Mr Meller, were you born in these parts?'

'No,' the forester answered without turning around.

'Where are you from, then?'

'Far away from here.'

'Been here long?'

'Long enough,' Meller turned and looked at the journalist.

'You had better keep your voice down or they'll hear us.'

'Who're they?'

'The Otarks, of course, who else? They'll hear us and pass the word on, or wait in ambush, jump us from behind, and tear us to bits ... And it would be much better if they didn't catch on why we're here.'

'Do things like that happen often? I've read in the papers that they seldom attack.' The forester didn't answer.

Betly involuntarily looked back over his shoulder.

'Can they shoot? Do they have arms of any kind? Rifles, or automatic machine-guns?'

'They rarely shoot. Their hands aren't made that way ... Aw heck, I meant their paws! They find it inconvenient to use arms of any kind.'

'Paws,' Betly echoed him. 'That means you don't look on them as human beings?'

'Who, us?'

'Yes, you. The local inhabitants.'

The forester spat.

'We sure don't. No one considers them human beings here.'

He spoke in chopped, curt phrases. But Betly had already forgotten his decision to curb his tongue.

'I say, have you ever spoken to them? Is it true they speak fluently?'

'The older ones do. The ones that were here when they had the research laboratory ... The younger ones don't speak as well. But they are more dangerous. Their heads are twice the size.' The forester suddenly pulled on the reins and brought his horse up short. There was a bitter note to his voice.

'Listen, all this talk won't do any good. It's no use. I've answered those questions dozens of times.'

'What's no use?'

'This trip we're making. It's no use. Everything's going to stay just as it is.'

'Why are you so sure? I'm from a big influential newspaper. We've got a lot of pull. We're collecting this material for the State Commission. If we can prove the Otarks are really so dangerous, drastic measures will be taken. You know, this time Army forces will be used against them.'

'It makes no difference, it won't do any good, anyway,' the forester sighed. 'You aren't the first one to come here. There's someone every year and all they're interested in are the Otarks. But you don't give a damn about the people that have to live with the Otarks. Everyone asks: "Is it true they can understand geometry?" ... Or, "Is it true they understand the theory of relativity?" As if that really means anything! As if that's reason enough not to destroy them!'

'But that's what I am here for,' Betly interrupted, 'to collect material for the commission. And then the whole country will be told ...'

'Do you think that the others who were here didn't collect material?' Meller broke in. 'Besides ... besides how can you understand what's going on here? You've got to live here to understand. It's one thing to come for a short stay, and it's quite another thing to live here all the time. Aw ...! What's the use of talking! Let's get going.' He touched his boots to his horse's flanks. 'Starting from here is where you usually find them. Down here in this valley.'

The journalist and the forester stood atop the slope. The path went winding down in an undulating zig-zag, seeming to drop from under the horses' hooves in perilous uncertainty.

Far away, down below, lay the bush-covered valley, cut across by a narrow, rocky stream. Straight from its banks rose a forest wall in steep ascent, and beyond it, in the boundless distance, the snow-whitened slopes of the mountain range.

From here the eye could take in the surrounding country

for miles around, but Betly could not see the slightest sign of life. There was not a single trail of chimney smoke or a stack of hay to indicate that the district was inhabited. It seemed as if the place were dead.

The sun hid behind a cloud and it became cold. The journalist suddenly felt that he had lost all wish to follow the forester down into the valley. He jerked his shoulders to shake off the chill. He thought of his warm, heated apartment, and the warm bright rooms of the editorial office. But then he took himself in hand. 'What nonsense! I've been in worse situations than this. What's there to be afraid of? I'm a good shot and I'm quick on the move. Who else could they have sent but me?' He saw Meller slipping his rifle off his shoulder and followed suit.

The mare was picking its way cautiously down the narrow path.

When they had finally gained level ground Meller said:

'Try to keep next to me. And better not talk. We've got to get to Steglik's farm by eight o'clock. We'll spend the night there.'

They gave rein to their horses and rode in complete silence for about two hours. They headed up the slope and skirted Mount Bear so that on their right hand they had a continuous wall of forest and on their left a precipice with an overgrowth of bushes so sparse and stunted they couldn't afford much of a hiding-place for anyone. They descended to the river and made their way along its rocky bottom until they reached an abandoned, asphalt road in a state of decay with grass growing through the cracks.

As soon as they were on the road Meller suddenly brought his horse to a halt and stood listening in tense alertness. He dismounted, got down on his knees and put his ear to the road.

'We're in trouble,' he said, as he straightened up. 'Someone's following close behind on horseback. Let's get off the road.'

Betly quickly dismounted and they led the horses behind a ditch among the alders.

About two minutes later the clatter of horse's hooves became clearly audible. The sound increased rapidly. You could feel that the horseman was riding his horse hard.

Then, through the leaves they saw a grey horse galloping for all it was worth, mounted by a man, dressed in yellow riding breeches and slicker, who sat his saddle with unpractised awkwardness. He passed by so near that Betly had a clear view of his face and realized that he had seen the man before. There had been a bunch of men around the bar in town yesterday evening – about five or six broad-shouldered, noisy fellows, dressed in loud-coloured clothes. What he remembered especially were their eyes – they were all the same. Lazy, hooded and brazenly insolent. Eyes like those, the journalist knew, belonged to gangsters.

The horseman had no sooner passed them than Meller sprung out onto the road.

'Hey!'

The man pulled at the reins and brought the horse to a stop.

'Hey, wait a minute!'

He looked hard at the forester and evidently recognized him. For several seconds they held each other's gaze. Then the man waved his hand, turned his horse and galloped on.

The forester followed him with his eyes until the sound of the horse's hooves died away in the distance. Then he whirled round with a groan and struck his head with his fist.

'Well, nothing's going to come of it now! That's for sure.'

'What's the matter?' Betly asked. He came out from his hiding place behind the bushes.

'Nothing... It's just that it won't work out now.'

'But why?' The journalist looked at the forester and was surprised to see tears in his eyes.

'Well, that's done it,' Meller said and turned away wiping his eyes with the back of his hand. 'Oh, the skunks! The dirty skunks!'

'Listen!' Betly was beginning to lose patience. 'If you're going to be so nervous I suppose there really is no sense in going on further.'

'Nervous!' the forester exclaimed. 'Me nervous? Is this what you call nervous? Look!'

He flung up his arm and pointed at the bough of a fir heavy with red-coloured cones, which hung over the road about thirty steps away.

Betly had no time to realize why he was supposed to look at it, when a shot rang out, powder smoke wafted into his face and the end cone dropped to the asphalt below.

'That's how nervous I am,' Meller said and went to the bushes for his horse.

They reached the farm as darkness was falling.

A tall, black-bearded man with a mop of unkempt hair came out of the unfinished log house and stood silently watching Betly and the forester as they unsaddled the horses. Then a red-headed woman, with a flat, expressionless face, whose hair was in the same state of untidiness, appeared on the porch. She was followed by three children, two boys of about eight and nine and a girl of thirteen, who was so thin she looked like a crooked line drawn on a piece of paper.

The five of them stood there showing neither surprise, joy, nor sorrow at the arrival of Meller and the journalist. They just stood there and looked. Betly didn't like this silent welcome in the least.

During supper he tried to pick up a conversation.

'I say, how do you get along with the Otarks? Do they bother you much?'

'What?' the black-bearded farmer said, and, putting his palm to his ear, bent across the table. 'What?' he shouted. 'Speak louder. I don't hear very well.'

This went on for several minutes with the farmer stubbornly refusing to understand what was wanted of him. At last he spread his arms wide and said, 'Sure the Otarks come around.' Did they bother him? No, personally they did not bother him. He couldn't say anything about other people because he didn't know. He didn't have anything to say.

In the middle of this enlightening conversation the thin little girl wrapped herself in a shawl and went out without saying a word to anyone.

As soon as the plates were emptied the farmer's wife brought two mattresses from the next room and began making up the beds for the travellers on the floor.

But Meller stopped her.

'I think we'd better spend the night in the shed.'

The woman straightened up without saying a word. The farmer quickly got up from the table.

'Why? I think you'd better sleep in the house.' But the forester had already doubled up the mattresses and was carrying them out.

The tall farmer lighted the way to the shed with a lantern. For a moment he stood watching as they arranged the mattresses and got ready for bed. An expression flitted across his face as though he were going to say something, but, as if on second thought, he just raised his hand and scratched his head. Then he went away.

'What was all that for?' Betly asked. 'Do you mean to say the Otarks get into the houses?'

Meller picked up a thick board from the ground and jammed it up against the heavy door, checking to see it wouldn't slip down.

'Let's go to bed,' he said. 'Anything can happen. They get into houses too.'

The journalist sat down on the mattress and began to unlace his boots.

'Are there any real bears left? I don't mean the Otarks,

but real wild bears. There used to be a lot of bears running wild in these forests.'

'Not a single one,' Meller answered. 'The first thing they did after they escaped from the laboratory on the island was to destroy all the real bears. The same thing happened to the wolves. There used to be racoons and foxes here as well as other forest animals. They got poison from the ruined laboratory and poisoned all the smaller animals. Wolves were lying dead all through the district ... for some reason they didn't eat the wolves. But they ate all the bears. They sometimes even eat each other.'

'Eat each other?'

'Sure. They're not human beings. You never know what to expect from them.'

'That means you consider they are just wild beasts?'

'No.' The forester shook his head. 'We don't consider them just wild beasts. It's only in the cities you argue about whether they are animals or men. We people here know they are neither the one nor the other. Before it was all very simple. There were people, and there were animals, and that's all. Now another species has appeared. The Otarks. It's the first time anything of the kind has happened since the world began. The Otarks are not just wild animals – it would be great if they were. But they aren't human beings, either.'

Although he realized the banality of the question he was going to ask, he couldn't help asking it.

'Is it true that they learn higher mathematics very easily?'

The forester turned on him as if shot from a catapult.

'Listen, will you shut up about higher mathematics! Just shut up! I don't give two hoots for anyone's knowledge of higher mathematics. Sure the Otarks find higher mathematics as easy as pie! So what ...? You've got to be a human being – that's what's important.'

He turned away and bit his lip.

'Nerves,' Betly thought to himself. 'He's got it bad. He's on the verge of a nervous breakdown.'

But the forester soon calmed down. He felt embarrassed for losing control of himself. After a short silence he said:

'Excuse me, but have you seen him personally?'

'Seen whom?'

'That genius. Fidler.'

'Fidler ...? Sure I've seen him. I talked to him just before I came out here. I interviewed him for the newspaper.'

'I suppose they keep him wrapped up in wax paper? So that a single drop of rain doesn't wet him.'

'Uh-huh. They sure do keep him well guarded.' Betly recalled how they had checked his pass and searched him the first time outside the wall surrounding the Science Centre. Then his pass had been checked again followed by another search – before he was allowed into the garden where Fidler came out to see him. They certainly did keep close watch over him. He really was a mathematical genius. He was only thirteen when he wrote his 'Changes in the general theory of relativity.' He'd have to be a genius for that.

'What does he look like?'

What does he look like?

The journalist became somewhat confused. He recalled Fidler as he had walked into the garden dressed in a white suit. There had been something clumsy and misshapen about his figure. He had wide hips, narrow shoulders and a short neck ... It had been a strange interview because Betly had had the feeling that he was the one that was being interviewed. Fidler answered his questions, of course, but he seemed to do it in a very flippant manner as if he were laughing at the journalist and at the whole world of ordinary people who lived out there beyond the wall of the Science Centre. He also asked the journalist questions. But they were idiotic questions, like whether Betly cared for carrot juice . . . as if he, Fidler, were carrying on an experimental study of an ordinary human being.

'Oh, he's average height,' Betly said. 'He's got little eyes ... But didn't you ever see him? He used to come to the laboratory here, on the lake.'

'He was here twice,' Meller answered, 'but he was guarded so closely that ordinary people couldn't come within a mile of him. At that time the Otarks were kept in an enclosure and Richard and Klein worked with them. They ate Klein up. After the Otarks escaped Fidler never showed up around here again ... What does he say about the Otarks now?'

'He says it was a very interesting scientific experiment. With great prospects. But he's not occupied with that problem at the moment. He's working on something connected with cosmic rays ...'

'But why was the whole thing started in the first place? What for?'

'Well, just how should I explain it ...?' Betly thought a moment. 'You see, it's this way in science: "What if?" A lot of discoveries have come from this.'

'What do you mean by, ' "What if?" '

'Well, take for instance: "What if we place a live wire in a magnetic field?" This "what if" gave us the electric motor ... In short, it just means experimenting.'

'Experimenting,' Meller ground his teeth on the word. 'They experimented and let cannibals out among the people. And now they've forgotten all about us. Fight your own battles as best you can, they say, Fidler doesn't care two pins about the Otarks now, or about us either. They're breeding in hundreds and no one knows what they've got up their sleeves or what plans they are hatching against us people.' He was silent for a while and then he sighed. 'When you think of what they've done, it's enough to make your hair stand on end! Imagine turning animals into people, and making them cleverer than people. Some of those people in the cities sure have gone daffy.'

He got up, took his loaded rifle and laid it down on the ground near his mattress.

'Listen, Mr Betly, if hell breaks loose, I mean if anybody starts banging on the door or tries to break it down you just stay put, just hug that mattress and keep your head down. Otherwise we'll shoot each other in the dark. You lay low ... I know what to do. I'm so used to this, I'm like a trained dog ... I wake up from instinct.'

In the morning when Betly walked out of the shed the sun was shining so bright and the grass and trees were so fresh after the rain that all that night talk seemed like horror stories.

The black-bearded man was already out working his field – his shirt a white spot on the other side of the river. For an instant the idea flitted across the journalist's mind that perhaps this was happiness – to rise with the sun, with no knowledge of the bustle and anxieties of city life, to know only the handle of your spade with its lump of brown earth.

But the forester quickly brought him back to reality. He appeared from around the shed with his rifle in his hand.

'Come here, I'll show you something.'

They skirted the shed and found themselves in the kitchen-garden facing the back of the house. Here Meller's behaviour astonished Betly. He sprinted past the bushes in a crouched position and squatted down in a ditch near the potato rows. He made a sign for the journalist to follow his example.

They began rounding the kitchen-garden, making their way along the ditch. Once they heard the woman's voice coming from the house, but they couldn't make out what she said.

Meller came to a stop.

'Look,' he said.

'At what?'

'You told me you were a hunter. Take a look!'

On a bare spot between the matted grass he saw a five-fingered imprint.

'Bear tracks?' Betly queried hopefully.

'Bear tracks? There haven't been any bears here for a helluva long time.'

'Then it was an Otark?'

The forester nodded.

'It's quite fresh,' the journalist whispered.

'Those tracks were made last night,' Meller said. 'See how damp they are. He was in the house before it began to rain.'

'In the house?' Betley felt his spine go cold as if he had come up against cold metal. 'You mean he was right in the house?'

The forester didn't answer, but ducked his head in the direction of the ditch and silently they made their way back.

When they reached the shed Meller waited until Betly got his breath back, and then said:

'That's the idea I got yesterday when we were at supper and Steglik pretended he couldn't hear well. He just wanted us to speak louder so that the Otark could catch what we were talking about. The Otark was hiding in the next room.'

The journalist felt that his voice had gone hoarse.

'What are you talking about? Do you mean to say that people unite with the Otarks? Against their own folks?'

'You better keep your voice down,' the forester said. 'What do you mean by "unite"? Steglik couldn't do anything else. The Otark just came and stayed. They often do that. An Otark can come into a house, for instance, go into the bedroom and lie down on the bed, and sleep the night. Sometimes he kicks the people out of the house for a day or two and lives in it himself.'

'But don't people do something about it? Why do they let them do such things? Why don't they shoot?'

'How are they going to shoot when there are other Otarks in the woods? The farmer has children and cattle that graze in the pastures, and a house that can burn ... down ... But the main thing is the children ... They can seize the children. You can't keep an eye on the little ones all the time. Besides they've taken all the rifles away from the farmers. That was at the very beginning. The very first year.'

'And the people gave them up?'

'What could they do? The ones that didn't were sorry afterwards ...'

He broke off suddenly and stared at the thicket of osier which grew about fifteen steps away.

Meller jerked his rifle to his shoulder and cocked the trigger. A huge brown hulk rose up, from which two evil eyes glared in fright, and a voice spoke out:

'Hey, don't shoot! Don't shoot!'

Instinctively the journalist grabbed Meller's shoulder. A shot thundered forth but the bullet only grazed a branch. The brown hulk doubled up, rolled off into the forest, and disappeared among the trees. For a few seconds all that could be heard was the snapping sound of breaking bushes, and then all was silent.

'What the holy devil!' The forester turned on him in a rage. 'What did you do that for?'

The journalist who had paled white as a sheet choked out in a whisper:

'He spoke like a human being. He begged you not to shoot.'

The forester looked at him for a moment, then his rage turned to tired indifference. He let his rifle down.

'Yes, I suppose ... The first time it does make an impression.'

There was a slight rustle behind them. They both whirled round.

The farmer's wife said:

'Come and have breakfast. I have already set the table.'

At the table everybody pretended that nothing had happened.

After breakfast the farmer helped them saddle the horses. They took their leave wordlessly.

When they had ridden off, Meller said:

'Listen, what are your plans? I didn't quite get it straight. I was told to guide you around the mountain side, and that's all.'

'Well, that's all ... That's all I want ... to ride about the mountains here. See the people ... talk to them. The more the better. Get acquainted with the Otarks, if possible. Sort of get a feel of the atmosphere.'

'Did you get a feel of the atmosphere back at that farm?'

Betly shrugged his shoulders.

The forester suddenly brought his horse up short.

'Quiet ...'

He was listening attentively.

'Someone's running this way. Something's happened at the farm.'

Betly had no time to get over his amazement at the forester's sense of hearing when someone shouted:

'Meller! Hey, Meller!'

They turned their horses, as the farmer ran up gasping for breath. He nearly fell as he grabbed for Meller's saddle horn.

'The Otark has taken Tina. He dragged her towards Moose canyon.'

He gasped for air, huge drops of sweat poured down his forehead.

With one huge swoop the forester had slung the farmer up on his saddle. His horse tore off at a swift gallop, the mud scattering high from under its flying hooves.

Betly could never have imagined that he would ever ride at such speed over such rugged terrain. He jumped pitfalls and the trunks of fallen trees, bushes and ditches rushed past in a blurred mosaic pattern. Somewhere along that frantic race a branch had torn off his cap, but he didn't even notice.

Of course, it really did not depend on him. His horse in the fierce heat of the race did its best to catch up with the roan. Betly had his arms tight around the mare's neck. He was certain he was going to be killed.

They galloped through the forest, across a huge meadow, went dashing down a slope, passed the farmer's wife and rode down into a large canyon.

Here the forester swung down from his horse, with the farmer bringing up the rear. He ran down a narrow path which led to a thicket of young spruce trees so sparsely placed you could see right through them.

The journalist also dismounted, threw the reins over the horse's neck and rushed after Meller. He ran after the forester; on the run he automatically thought of how amazingly the latter had changed. Nothing remained of his former apathy and indecisiveness. His movements were light and collected. Without a moment's thought he changed directions, jumped over pits, crawled under low-lying branches. He rushed on as if the Otark's tracks had been chalked for him in a big thick line.

For a while Betly managed to keep up with the headlong speed of the pursuers, but gradually he began to lag behind. His heart was thumping in his chest ... his throat burned and he felt he was choking. He slowed down to a walk and for some minutes wandered around all by himself. Then he heard voices.

At the spot where the canyon narrowed down, the forester was standing in front of a thick nut-grove with his rifle raised and trigger cocked, ready to shoot. The girl's father was standing nearby.

The forester spoke out spacing his words slowly:

'Let her go or I shall kill you.'

He directed his words towards the nut-grove.

A growl was his only answer intermingled with the crying of a child.

The forester repeated his words.

'Let her go or I will kill you. I will track you down, even if I die doing it. You know me.'

There was more growling and then a voice spoke out, but it wasn't human ... more like a gramophone record that sort of ran all the words together.

'If I let her go, you won't kill me?'

'No,' Meller said. 'If you let her go, I won't touch you.'

There was silence in the thicket, except for the whimpering of the child.

Then there was the sound of twigs snapping and something white fluttered for a moment in the bushes. The thin little girl made her appearance. One of her hands was bloody. She supported it with her other hand.

Whimpering she passed the three men without turning her head, and with small staggering steps made her way to the house.

The three men followed her with their eyes.

The black-bearded farmer looked at Meller and Betly. In his wide-open eyes there was something so sharp and cutting that the journalist could not stand his gaze and dropped his eyes.

'There you are,' the farmer said.

They spent the night in an empty little hut in the forest. It was only a few hours' ride to the island on the lake where the laboratory had once been, but Meller refused to travel in the dark.

It was their fourth day on the road and the journalist felt that his well tried optimism was beginning to give way. Formerly whenever he came up against any unpleasantness or trouble he always had a pet phrase. 'No matter what, life sure is a wonderful thing.' But now he realized that was all right if you are travelling in a comfortable train from one town to another or walking through the glass door of an hotel to meet some famous personage. But it just didn't do for the kind of thing that had happened to Steglik, for instance.

The whole district seemed to be stricken with some incurable ailment. The people were apathetic and unsociable. Even the children never laughed.

Once he asked Meller why the farmers did not leave the place. Meller explained that all they had was the land that belonged to them. But they couldn't even sell that. Nobody wanted it because of the Otarks.

Betly asked him:

'Why don't you leave?'

The forester had thought a moment, then pressed his lips together.

'I suppose it's because I'm of some use here. The Otarks are afraid of me. I don't have anything of my own. No family. No house. They can't put pressure on me in any way. The only thing they can do is fight me. And that's risky.'

'That means they respect you.'

Meller raised his head, and looked at the journalist in perplexity.

'The Otarks? ... Oh, no! They don't know what respect means. They are not human beings. They can only be afraid. They are afraid of me because I kill them.'

But it seemed that the Otarks were ready to take a certain amount of risk. Both the forester and the journalist felt that. They were under the impression that they were gradually being enclosed on all sides. Three times they had been shot at. Once from the window of an abandoned house and twice straight from the forest. After each attack they had discovered bear tracks. The number of tracks increased with every day ...

In the hut they made a fire in the little stone fireplace and cooked themselves some supper. The forester lit his pipe and sat looking at the fire with a sorrowful expression on his face.

They had left the horses standing in front of the open door of the hut.

The journalist looked at the forester. His respect for this man had grown every day they were together. Meller had had no education, he had spent his whole life in the forest, he hardly ever read anything, and two minutes would have been more than enough to speak on a topic like art. Nevertheless the journalist felt that he would never have wanted a better friend. His ideas were always sensible and independent. If he had nothing to say he kept silent. At the beginning the journalist had thought him nervous and irritably weak, but now Betly understood that this was all because of his deep bitterness for the people of this large abandoned district, which, thanks to scientific experimentation, was in such grievous trouble.

The last two days Meller had been quite ill. He had swamp fever. His face was all covered with red spots from the high temperature.

The fire was dying down in the fireplace. The forester suddenly asked:

'Is he young?'

'Who?'

'That scientist. I mean Fidler.'

'Yes,' the journalist answered. 'He must be about thirty. No more. Why?'

'That's bad. It's bad that he's young,' the forester said.

'Why?'

Meller was silent for a while.

'You see, they take the talented people and put them in secluded surroundings. They pet and pamper them. And of course they have no idea of what real life is like. That's why they have no feelings for people.' He sighed deeply. 'You've got to be a human being first ... and then you can be a scientist.'

He got up.

'It's time to go to bed. We'll have to take turns or the Otarks will kill the horses.' It was the journalist's turn to stand watch first.

The horses were munching hay from a small stack that had been left there from last year.

He sat down on the doorstep of the hut and placed his gun between his knees.

The darkness fell quickly as if a blanket had been placed over everything. His eyes gradually became accustomed to the gloom. Then the moon came out. The sky was clear and starry. A flight of little birds, calling to each other, passed high overhead. Contrary to the big birds, they migrated at night for safety's sake, in fear of falling prey to the big birds.

Betly got up and walked around the hut. The clearing where the little hut stood was tightly surrounded by forest on all sides, and this was dangerous. The journalist checked his trigger to see that it was cocked.

He began to go back over the events of the last few days, the conversations, the faces, and thought of all he would have to tell about the Otarks when he got back to the office. Then another thought struck him: come to think of it the thought of his return home was always present in his subconscious mind and of course lent a certain colouring to everything that had taken place. Even when they were chasing the Otark who had taken the little girl, Betly never forgot that no matter how horrible it was here, he could always return home and get away from it all.

'I'll be able to get away from all this horror,' he said to himself. 'But what about Meller? And all the others . . .?'

But this thought was too gloomy and he didn't want to think it through to the end.

He sat down in the shadow of the hut and began thinking of the Otarks. He recalled the heading of an article in one of the newspapers: 'Reason without Kindness.' This article was close to what the forester had said. He did not consider the Otarks human beings because they had no 'compassion', no feeling for others. 'Reason without kindness.' But was that possible? Could reason exist without kindness? What came first? Isn't kindness the logical effect of reasoning? Or was it the other way around ...? It had already been established that the Otarks were more capable of logical reasoning than people, that they understood abstraction and abstract quantity and remembered it all much better than people.

He remembered that one of the farmers had told him and Meller that he had seen a practically naked Otark with hardly any fur on him at all, and the forester had said that the Otarks were becoming more and more like people all the time. Was it possible that they would one day conquer the world? Was reason without kindness stronger than the reason of a human being?

'But that won't be very soon,' he said to himself. 'Even if it does happen, I'll have lived my life and will be dead by that time, anyway.'

But what about the children? What kind of a world would they live in ...!

In a world of Otarks or a world of inhuman sybernetic robots which some people considered cleverer than people?

His son suddenly appeared before him and spoke out:

'Papa, listen. We are ... we, isn't that so? And they ... are they. But they also think about themselves as ... "we", don't they?'

'You grow up too quickly,' Betly thought to himself. 'When I was seven I didn't ask such questions.'

Somewhere in back a twig snapped. The boy disappeared.

The journalist looked around in alarm and listened attentively.

Everything seemed to be all right.

A bat crossed the clearing in a slanting trembling flight.

He straightened up. The thought suddenly struck Betly that the forester was keeping something back from him. He had never told him anything about the rider who had galloped after them on that abandoned road.

He sat down again with his back to the wall of the hut.

His son appeared in front of him again with another question:

'Papa, where did everything come from? The trees, and the houses, and air and people? Where did everything come from?'

He began telling the boy about the evolution of the Universe, then as though a knife had stabbed him, he woke up.

The moon had gone, but the sky had become lighter.

The horses weren't on the clearing any longer. That is, one of them wasn't there any longer, but the other was lying on its side and three grey shadows were pottering around it. One of the shadows straightened up and the journalist saw a huge Otark with a large heavy head, wide open jaws and eyes that glittered in the semi-darkness.

Somewhere nearby he heard a whisper:

'He's sleeping.'

'No, he is already awake.'

'Go up to him.'

'He'll shoot.'

'He would have shot before now if he could. He's either asleep or he's paralysed with fear. Go on.'

The journalist had really lost all capability of movement. It seemed to be all happening in a dream. He realized that what had taken place was irreparable, that disaster had arrived, but he couldn't move a hand or foot.

The whispering went on:

'What about the other one? He'll shoot.'

'He's sick. He won't wake up . . . Go on . . . !'

With a colossal effort Betly managed to slant his eyes. An Otark was round the corner of the hut. He was small and looked like a pig.

Overcoming his shocked immobility the journalist pressed the trigger. Two shots thundered out one after the other, and two case-shots flew skywards.

Betly sprung up and his rifle dropped out of his hands.

He rushed into the hut trembling, banged it shut behind him and slipped the latch in place.

The forester stood with his rifle ready to fire. His lips moved. The journalist felt rather than heard the question:

'The horses?'

He nodded.

A rustling sound was heard outside the door. The Otarks were propping something up against the door from the outside.

A voice called out:

'Hey, Meller! Hey!'

The forester dashed to the window and wanted to stick out his rifle. At that very instant the shadow of a black paw flashed out across the background of the brightened sky; he hardly had time to pull his rifle back.

This was followed by satisfied laughter from outside.

A dragging gramophone voice called out:

'This is the end for you Meller.'

Other voices broke in interrupting the first:

'Meller, Meller, speak to us ...'

'Hey, forester, say something clever. You're a human being, you've got to be clever ...'

'Meller, say something and I'll prove you're wrong ...'

'Say something, Meller. Call me by name. I'm Philip.'

The forester kept silent.

The journalist took several uncertain steps towards the window. The voices were very close, right behind the log wall of the hut. The air reeked of animal stench – a mixture of blood, dung and something else.

The Otark that had called itself Philip spoke out from right under the window:

'You're a journalist, hey? You're right near the window, hey ...?'

The journalist cleared his throat. It was parched dry.

The same voice asked:

'What did you come here for?'

It became very quiet.

'You came here to kill us?'

It was quiet again for a moment and then a hubbub of excited voices burst forth.

'Sure, they want to kill us ... They made us, and now they want to kill us all off ...'

There was the sound of growling followed by a bedlam of noise. The journalist got the impression that the Otarks had begun a fight.

Then the voice of the one who had called himself Philip called out again:

'Hey, forester, why don't you shoot? You always shoot. Why don't you shoot now? Say something.'

All of a sudden a shot rang out from somewhere.

Betly turned round.

The forester had climbed up on the fireplace, had moved aside the straw-covered laths that the roof was made of, and was shooting.

Two shots rang out. He recharged his rifle and shot again.

The Otarks scattered helter-skelter, as fast as they could.

Meller jumped down from the fireplace.

'We've got to get hold of some horses or it's going to be pretty rough going.'

They examined the three Otarks that he had shot.

One of them, who was quite young, was practically hairless. There was only a tuft of fur growing at the nape of his neck. Betly nearly vomited when Meller turned his face upward on the grass.

The forester said:

'You've got to remember that they are not human beings, although they can speak. They eat people. And they eat each other too.'

The journalist looked around. It was already light. There was the clearing and the forest and the dead Otarks – for a moment it all seemed unreal.

Could this be possible? ... Could this be he, Donald Betly standing here? ...

'This is where Klein was eaten by an Otark,' Meller said. 'One of our local men told us about it. He worked here as janitor, doing odd jobs when the laboratory was in full swing. He happened to be in the next room that evening and he heard everything ...'

The journalist and the forester were now on the island, in the main building of the Science Centre. In the morning they had removed the saddles from the dead horses and crossed over to the island on the dam. They had only one rifle now. The Otarks had taken Betly's along with them when they ran away. Meller planned on reaching the nearest farm while it was still daylight and getting some horses there. But the journalist had talked him into giving him a half hour to look over the abandoned laboratory.

'He heard everything,' the forester went on. 'It happened about nine o'clock in the evening. Klein had some sort of a contraption that he was taking apart. He was messing around with some electric wires and talking to the Otark who was sitting on the floor. They were discussing something connected with physics. That Otark was one of the first that they had bred and was considered one of the cleverest. He could even speak foreign languages ... Our local chap was scrubbing the floor in the next room and heard them talking. Then there was silence for a while, followed by the sound of something heavy falling. And suddenly he heard someone say: 'Oh, my God ...!' That was Klein. There was such horror in his voice that the chap's knees buckled under. And then there was a terrible cry and Klein screaming 'Help! Help!' The janitor opened the door and looked in. Klein was thrashing around on the floor and the Otark was gnawing and chewing at him. The janitor was so paralysed with shock and fear that he just stood there. He only managed to bang the door shut when the Otark went for him.

'What happened after that?'

'They killed two other laboratory assistants and ran away. About five or six Otarks stayed on as if nothing had happened. When the commission from the city came they talked to them and took the Otarks back to the city. Later we heard that they ate another man in the train ...'

Everything had remained untouched in the large room of the laboratory. There were dishes on the long tables, all covered with a thick layer of dust, spiders had spun their webs all through the wires of the X-ray apparatus. But the windows were broken and the acacia trees, now growing wild, had thrust their branches through the shattered glass.

Meller and the journalist left the main building.

Betly wanted to see the radiation installation and begged for another five minutes.

The asphalt on the main street of the settlement was overgrown with grass and young tenacious bushes. The autumn leanness of the trees made it possible to see clearly for some distance. There was a smell of rotting leaves and damp trees.

On the square Meller suddenly stopped short.

'Did you hear anything?'

'No,' Betly answered.

'You know, I keep on thinking of how they ambushed us in the hut in a united group,' the forester said. 'That never happened before. They've always attacked individually.'

He stopped to listen again.

'They could surprise us nicely here. We'd better get out of the place as quickly as possible.'

They reached a low built round-shaped building with narrow, barred windows. The heavy, massive door stood slightly ajar. The concrete floor near the doorstep was covered with a thin carpet of rubbish from the forest – rust-coloured pine-needles, dust, and myriads of wings from all kinds of insects.

Cautiously they entered the first room with an

overhanging ceiling. Another massive door led into a low-ceilinged hall.

They looked in. A squirrel with a bushy tail, like a flame, flashed across the wooden table and sprang out of the window through the bars.

For a second the forester eyed its flight. Then tensed, in alert listening, his rifle grasped tightly in his hands.

'This won't do at all,' he said, and swiftly turned back the way they had come.

But it was too late.

There was a rustling sound from outside, and the entrance door clanged shut. Then something heavy was placed against it.

For one second Meller and the journalist looked at each other, then rushed for the window.

Betly took one look and staggered back.

The square, and the wide, dried-out pool, built for no apparent reason, was swarming with Otarks There were dozens and dozens of them and they kept on coming and coming as if they were gushing up from underground. The noise and hubbub sounded like all hell let loose – the sounds were neither human nor animal like – a mixture of growls and cries.

The forester and Betly stood shocked into dumbness.

A young Otark was standing nearby on its hind legs. It was holding something round in its paws.

'He's holding a stone,' the journalist whispered, still not able to believe what had happened. 'He wants to throw a stone in through the window.' But it wasn't a stone.

The round object flew through the air; near the window bars it burst out in a blinding light and bitter smoke wafted in on all sides.

The forester staggered back from the window. There was an expression of bewilderment on his face.

His rifle fell out of his hands and he grabbed at his chest.

'Oh, the devils!' he said and raised his hand and looked at

his bloody fingers. 'The dirty devils! They've got me at last!'

Pale as death, he took two faltering steps and crouched down on his heels, then slid to the floor with his back up against the wall.

'They got me!'

'No!' Betly screamed. 'No!' He was shaking like in a fever.

Meller bit his lips, and raised his bloodless face to him.

'The door!'

The journalist ran towards the entrance door. Something heavy outside was being moved away.

Betly pushed the two bolts into place. It was lucky that the door had been built so that it could be strongly locked from within.

He went back to the forester.

Meller was now lying near the wall with his hands pressed to his chest. A large red spot had spread over his shirt. He wouldn't let the journalist try to staunch the wound.

'It won't help anyway,' he said. 'I feel it's the end. I don't want the extra pain. Just leave me alone.'

'But help will come!' Betly cried out.

'From where?'

The question was so blunt and hopeless, that the journalist went cold. They were silent for a while. Then the forester said:

'Do you remember the horseman we saw the first day we set out?'

'Yes.'

'He was most likely on his way to warn the Otarks of our coming. They've got some sort of link-up ... the bandits from the city and the Otarks here. That's how they got organized. There's no need to be surprised. I'm quite sure that if octopuses were to come here from Mars there would be people who would come to an understanding with them.'

'That's true,' the journalist whispered.

The time dragged on without any change till evening. Meller was noticeably weakening. But the haemorrhage had stopped. He hadn't allowed the journalist to touch him. They both sat, side by side, on the stone floor.

The Otarks didn't bother them. Nor was there any attempt to break in the door or throw another hand-grenade. The clamour outside died down from time to time, then rose again.

When the sun had set and it became cooler the forester asked for a drink of water. The journalist gave him some water from the flask he carried and wet his face.

The forester said:

'Perhaps it's just as well that the Otarks have appeared in this world. Perhaps people will now be able to clearly define what it means to be a human being. Perhaps they will now understand that it is not enough for a creature to be able to do sums and solve problems in geometry to be considered a human being. They'll have to learn it requires something much more than that. Those scientists have grown very proud and can't see further than their experiments. But science isn't everything.'

Meller died during the night. The journalist lived for three more days.

The first day he thought only of how to escape. He passed from desperation to hope, and several times he fired his rifle through the window thinking that someone might hear the sound of the shots and come and save him.

By night time he understood that all his hopes were in vain. His life seemed to be divided into two disconnected parts. What bothered him most was that the two parts were not connected by any logic or continuity. One part belonged to the prosperous, rational life of a successful journalist which had ended when he had ridden off with Meller to the forest-covered mountains of the Main Mountain Range. There had been no indication whatsoever in that first life of his that he would have to die here in the abandoned laboratory on this island.

The second part was composed of probabilities and improbabilities. It was all made up of chance happenings. And there had been no need for it to happen. It had been up to him to decide whether to come here or go somewhere else. Instead of coming here for information on the Otarks, he could have flown to Nubio and written an article on the excavation of ancient monuments of Egyptian art.

Absurd fortuity had brought him here. And that thought was the most horrible of all.

Several times he even stopped believing that this had happened to him. When this happened he would begin walking around the hall, touching the walls lit up by the sunlight, and the dust-covered tables.

The Otarks seemed to have lost all interest in him. There were very few of them left on the square and in the pool. Sometimes they would begin to fight among themselves, and once Betly saw with a sinking heart how they all turned on one of their own, tore him to bits and ate him up.

During the night he suddenly felt that Meller was to blame for his predicament. He felt such repugnance towards the dead forester, that he dragged his body to the next hall right up to the door.

For an hour or two afterwards he sat on the floor and repeated over and over again:

'My God, why did it have to be me? ... Why did it have to be me ...?'

On the second day the Otarks came up to the window several times and tried to get him to speak. But he wouldn't answer.

One of the Otarks said:

'Hey, you, journalist. Come on out. We won't hurt you.'

Another Otark standing nearby laughed.

Again Betly's thoughts turned to the forester. But now he no longer felt as he had. He decided that the forester was a hero. The only real hero that Betly had ever come across. All alone, without assistance from anyone, he had fought against the Otarks, had defied them, and had died undefeated.

On the third day the journalist fell into delirium. He imagined that he was back at the office, dictating to the stenographer.

The article went under the heading: What is a Human Being?

He dictated very loudly:

'In this century of amazing developments in science, one might conclude that science is all powerful. But let us try to imagine that an artificial brain has been created which is far superior to the human brain, possessing greater capacity for work. Will a creature with a brain of this kind have the right to be called a human being? What really makes us what we are? The ability to count, to analyse, to make logical computations, or is it something else that has been bred by society, something to do with people's relations to each other and the attitude of the individual to a collective body? If we take the Otarks, for instance ...'

But his thoughts were all in a jumble ...

On the third day there was an explosion. Betly came to himself.

He thought that he had sprung up and was standing with his gun ready to shoot. In reality he was lying on the floor near the wall, quite helpless and too weak to even move.

The muzzle of a beast appeared in front of him. With agonizing effort he strained his brain and suddenly remembered what Fidler looked like. Like an Otark!

Then that thought was crushed and became all mixed up. Already feeling that the Otark was tearing at his living flesh, in the course of a tenth part of a second Betly still had time to think that the Otarks were really not such a great menace, that there were only a few hundred of them in this abandoned district. That they would be overcome. But people . . . ! Where were the people . . . !

He could not know, of course, that news of Meller's disappearance had swept throughout the whole district and that the farmers, reduced to despair, were digging rifles up out of hidden caches.

Arkady and Boris Strugatsky

'... Scientists inform us of interstellar plankton, of the existence of spores of unknown life in space. Extensive accumulations of such spores are found only beyond the orbit of Mars. Their origin has not yet been determined ...'

AN EMERGENCY CASE

VICTOR BORISOVICH had been disappointed in Titan. The small planet revolved too rapidly and had a dark, unsettled atmosphere. He was intrigued, however, with Saturn's rings and the strange play of colours on its surface. The inter-planetary spaceship had unloaded food, liquefied deuterium and cybernetic equipment for the planetologists, and had immediately started on its return journey, taking twenty-eight tons of erbium and biologist Malyshev on board.

When passing through the asteroid zone, the spaceship lost speed and deviated from its course. It was the usual thing. They had a bad time of it. Everyone was exhausted and Malyshev most of all. The poor chap could not stand overstrain. When they pulled him out of the shock absorber, he was as yellow as a lemon. He felt himself all over, shook his head and made for his cabin without saying a word. He was in a hurry to see how the overstrain had affected his snail – a fat blue slug with a multivalvular shell caught in the oil ocean near Erbium Valley.

Now, like everything else in this world, good or bad, the journey was coming to an end. In less than a day the spaceship would land at the rocket airfield in Lomonosov Crater, then a week in quarantine and at last – the Earth. Six months on vacation – sunshine, a blue sea, green meadows and rustling pine-trees …

Victor Borisovich smiled, turned on his side and yawned. There were still two hours to go before his turn. Toomer was still doing his watch. Victor Borisovich pictured Toomer with his long nose, thin as a stick, hunched over the computer, reading the blue recording tape of the control system. Then Toomer's image faded into a rough moss-covered boulder. There was deep water under the boulder and if one strained one's eyes one could see a black-backed pike hiding among the weeds . . . Suddenly a bumble-bee began to buzz in his ear. Victor Borisovich started, and woke up. It was dark in the cabin. He could hear a bumble-bee quite close to him.

'It can't be,' said Victor Borisovich, confidently.

He got up and switched on the lamp. The buzzing stopped. Victor Borisovich looked around and saw a black spot on the bedclothes. It wasn't a bumble-bee. It was a fly.

'Good Lord!' he exclaimed.

The fly didn't move. It was quite black, with black widespread wings. Victor Borisovich took aim carefully and snatched it. He lifted his clenched fist to his ear and listened. Something was fluttering inside in a very familiar way.

A fly! A fly on board the spaceship! He looked at his hand in amazement. 'Just imagine! I must show it to Toomer.'

With his free hand Victor Borisovich pulled on his trousers. Then he rushed into the corridor and along to the chart-room.

Toomer was standing in the chart-room watching the screen of the television projector where two narrow crescents, one of the Moon and the other of the Earth, were rocking slightly.

'Hello, Toom,' said Victor Borisovich.

Toomer nodded and looked at him with his deep-set eyes.

'Guess what I've got here,' said Victor Borisovich, slightly shaking his fist.

'An airship,' answered Toomer ironically.

'No, it's not an airship,' said Victor Borisovich, 'it's a fly. A living fly, you old fathead.'

Toomer looked bored. He said:

'The ferrite accumulator isn't working well.'

'I'll replace it,' said Victor Borisovich, 'you see, the thing woke me up. It hums like a bumble-bee in a flower-bed.'

'It wouldn't have woken me up,' said Toomer, through clenched teeth.

'It's fluttering, the pet,' said the navigator lovingly.

Toomer looked at him. Victor Borisovich sat holding his fist to his ear, smiling happily. 'Victor,' said Toomer reprovingly. 'What a face you've got!'

Konstantin Yefremovich Stankevich, captain of the spaceship, entered the chart-room followed by air engineer Lidin.

'I told you he wasn't sleeping,' said Lidin, pointing at the navigator.

'Something's happened to him,' said Toomer sarcastically. 'Just look at his face.'

'I've caught a fly,' explained Victor Borisovich.

'You don't say!' said Lidin, greatly surprised.

'I'm going to bed, Konstantin Yefremovich,' said Toomer, 'Victor, take over, there's a good chap.'

'Wait a minute,' said Victor Borisovich.

'Let me see what you've got there,' demanded Lidin. He looked as if he had never seen a fly in his life.

Victor Borisovich unclenched his fist a little and cautiously passed two fingers of his left hand inside. He pulled out the fly by its legs.

'How could a fly have got into the spaceship?' mused the captain. 'By the way, Victor Borisovich, you are responsible!'

The navigator was also the ship's sanitary officer.

'That's it,' said Toomer. 'Breeding flies on the spaceship,

while the ferrite accumulator is completely out of order. It's your turn for the watch.'

'Not yet,' said the navigator, 'I still have ten minutes left. I must show it to Malyshev. He hasn't seen a fly for a long time either.'

He moved towards the door, carrying the fly in front of him as if it were a plate of soup.

'Fly-catcher,' said Toomer contemptuously.

The captain laughed. Suddenly the door opened and Malyshev entered the room. The navigator jumped aside.

'Careful!' he said angrily.

Malyshev apologized. He had a dishevelled and rather embarrassed appearance.

'The fact is ...' he began, and stopped suddenly on seeing the fly. 'May I?' he asked, holding out his hand.

'A living fly!' said Victor Borisovich proudly. Malyshev held the insect by its wing and its buzzing filled the room.

'It's got eight legs,' said Malyshev slowly.

'And what of it?' said Toomer. 'Victor, take over. It's time now.'

'It's not a fly,' said Malyshev, raising his eyebrow. 'My first thought was that it might be a "mourning cloak" – antrax morio, but it isn't. It's not a fly at all.'

'Then what is it?' asked the navigator, somewhat piqued.

'Listen,' said Malyshev. 'Have you got any disinsectors? And I'll need a microscope.'

'But what's the matter?' asked the navigator.

The captain frowned and came up to them. Lidin also drew nearer.

'Listen,' repeated Malyshev. 'I want a microscope. Let's go to my cabin. I'll show you something interesting.'

'Don't drop the fly,' Toomer called out after them.

When they were passing down the corridor, Lidin suddenly cried: 'Another fly!' They saw a fly crawling on the wall near the ceiling. It was black, with black wide-spread wings.

In the biologist's cabin there were three of them. One was sitting on the pillow, while two were crawling on the walls of the glass tank containing the blue slug. Lidin entering last, banged the door, and the flies rose into the air making a noise like a swarm of bumble-bees.

'F-f-funny flies,' said Victor Borisovich uncertainly, and he looked at Stankevich.

The captain stood still, watching the flies. He was getting red in the face.

'It's a nasty business,' he said at last.

'What's wrong?' asked Lidin. Malyshev looked sullen.

'You heard me say – they aren't flies. Not the flies we're used to on Earth. Don't you see?'

'Good Lord!' said Victor Borisovich and wiped his right hand on his shirt.

'Then that's it,' said Lidin. A black fly flew in front of his eyes and he recoiled, hitting the back of his head against the closed door. 'Get away!' he cried waving his hands convulsively.

'We need some kind of disinsector,' said the Captain. 'What have we got on board?'

' "Lethal",' answered the navigator.

'What else?'

'That's all.'

'All right,' said the captain, 'I'll attend to the matter myself. Go and wash your hands and rub them with formalin.'

Malyshev was still examining the fly, holding it close to his nose. Victor Borisovich noticed that his fingers were trembling.

'Throw the filthy thing away,' said Lidin. He was standing in the corridor and looking around him every now and then.

'I'll need it,' answered Malyshev, 'you aren't going to catch me another one, are you?'

In the bathroom Victor Borisovich hurriedly doffed his

shirt, threw it into the rubbish chute and rushed over to the washbasin. He washed his hands with soap, rubbed them with a sponge, then again with soap ... They became red and swollen, but he went on rubbing and rubbing.

The most terrible thing that can ever happen on a spaceship had occurred. It is very seldom that such things come to pass, but it would be better if they never happened at all. A spaceship has very thick walls and everything that penetrates through them means mortal danger, be it a meteorite, cosmic radiation, or eight-legged flies. Flies are especially dangerous. Three years before, Victor Borisovich had taken part in a rescue expedition on Callisto. The party consisted of five people, two pilots and three scientists, and they happened to bring some plasma from that poisonous little planet onto the ship. The corridors of the ship were all covered with a transparent sticky web, something squelched under one's feet, and captain Rudolph Tserer lay pale and motionless in an armchair in the chart-room with tiny lilac-coloured spiders crawling all over his face ...

Victor Borisovich rubbed his swollen hands with formalin and went out into the corridor. Flies were crawling on the ceiling. There were about twenty of them. Lidin appeared, his face contorted.

'Where do they come from,' he asked hoarsely, 'the loathsome creatures?'

A buzzing fly flew up from beneath his feet, and he stopped abruptly, raising his clenched fists above his head. 'Order!' said Victor Borisovich, 'Order, air engineer! Where are you going?'

'To wash.'

'What about the disinsector?'

Lidin only grimaced and went quietly into the bathroom. Victor Borisovich went to his cabin, slipped on a fresh shirt and jacket and set off back to the chart-room. A swarm of black midges brushed past his face with a thin buzzing sound.

On a table in front of the chart-room computer stood a bottle containing a turbid liquid that produced a repulsive smell even through the stopper. A fly was swimming in the liquid. Probably Malyshev had crushed its wings so that it couldn't take off. From time to time it hummed loudly.

Toomer and Malyshev stood at the table, watching it closely. Victor Borisovich joined them.

The liquid inside the bottle was 'Lethal'. It was supposed to kill insects instantly and could even kill an ox. But the eight-legged fly evidently knew nothing about the matter and continued swimming in the disinsector, buzzing angrily from time to time.

'Five and a half minutes,' said Toomer. 'It's time you gave it up, deary.'

'Maybe there is some other kind of disinsector?' asked Malyshev.

Victor Borisovich shook his head. He examined the ceiling. There were no flies yet in the chart-room. Then he noticed Toomer who was looking sarcastically at Victor's bloated hands. Victor Borisovich thrust his hands into his pockets and moaned with pain.

'All for nothing,' he thought, 'the creature isn't even afraid of "Lethal". A cubic centimetre of the liquid to each square metre of surface. Destroys all kinds of insects, their larvae and eggs.' He looked again at the fly in the bottle. It was still swimming, and its humming was extremely annoying. Victor Borisovich sighed, took his hands out of his pockets and said:

'Go off watch, Toom.'

He took over the watch and reported to the captain. Stankevich nodded absently.

'Where is Lidin?' he asked.

'Washing.'

'Disinfecting himself,' added Toomer.

'Right!' said the captain, 'you will all put on protective

suits, and get yourselves vaccinated against sand-fever. The next thing. "Lethal" is no good. But maybe it is still possible to treat the flies with something else. What's your opinion, Comrade Malyshev?'

'I beg your pardon?' said Malyshev absently. He drew himself away from the fly in the bottle and hurriedly added: 'Yes, yes, quite possible.'

'We've got Petronal, Buxil, Nitrosylicol ... liquefied gases ...'

'Our own spit,' said Toomer in a low voice.

Stankevich glanced at him coldly.

'It's no time for jokes, Toomer,' he said. 'We shall carry out the tests in the medical department. Are you ready to help me, Comrade Malyshev?'

'At your service,' answered Malyshev, 'but I want a microscope.'

'The microscope is in the medical department. You will stay here, Victor Borisovich. They'll bring you a suit straight away.'

'Very good, Captain,' said Victor Borisovich. A loud buzzing began. Everyone looked at the bottle and then immediately swung their eyes up to the ceiling. A large black fly was sitting there, buzzing triumphantly.

Toomer brought Victor Borisovich a protective suit. He quickly opened the door, jumped like a billy-goat over the coaming and slammed the door behind him.

For a moment the chart-room was filled with a loud humming and buzzing. Toomer removed the spectrolyte cap from his head.

'The corridor is swarming with flies, so that you can hardly walk,' he said. 'Roll up your sleeve.'

He took the syringe and gave the navigator a shot of anti-sand-fever serum. Sand-fever was the only infectious space disease against which an antidote had been discovered. There was clearly no sense in inoculating against it as the only place where sand-fever bacilli had been found was Venus, but the captain did not want to take any chances.

'How are the others getting on?' asked Victor Borisovich, rolling down his sleeve.

'Kosty's as angry as blazes,' said Toomer. 'Nothing seems to affect the flies. Malyshev is delighted and keeps on cutting up the flies into little pieces and examining them under the microscope. He says he has never seen anything like it. He says they have neither eyes, nor mouth, nor gullet, nor anything else. He can't understand how they multiply ...'

'But can he tell where they come from?'

'He says that they must be the spores of some unknown form of life that must have been floating in space for millions of years and have finally found favourable conditions on our ship. He says we are extremely lucky; no such cases have been reported before.'

'Wandering life,' said the navigator putting on his protective suit. 'I've heard about it. But somehow I find it hard to consider us as being lucky. By the way, how could they have got into the ship?'

'Remember Lidin getting out a week ago? If I'm not mistaken it was in the asteroid belt.'

'Or maybe they got in from Titan?'

Toomer shrugged his shoulders.

'Malyshev says that there are no eight-legged flies on Titan. It doesn't make any difference though. Thank God they aren't wasps.'

Toomer jumped over the coaming again and closed the door behind him. Victor Borisovich sat down at the control panel. Dressed in a protective suit and wearing a spectrolyte cover over his head he felt himself completely safe, and even started humming a tune. Dozens of flies were now circling just below the ceiling, some were flying in front of the television screen, others crawled on the record tape of the control system. But thanks to the sound-proof protective suit he could no longer hear their buzzing. Victor Borisovich examined the control panel. There was a fly at his elbow. He took aim and slapped it with his gloved hand. The fly rolled over, waved its legs and then lay still. Victor Borisovich bent over it and examined it carefully. A dead black fly with eight legs . . . A nasty creature, no doubt, but why were they so dangerous? No insect is dangerous in itself; it is the infection or poison that it carries that is dangerous. These may still turn out to be neither infectious nor poisonous. However, if even one of these cosmic flies were to get to Earth, one could hardly imagine the consequences ...

The navigator turned round. A sheet of paper from the table had fallen to the floor and was now floating towards the door. The door into the corridor was ajar.

'Hey, who's there?' cried Victor Borisovich, 'close the door, please!'

He waited for a moment, then rose and went out into the corridor. Flies were crawling and flying all over the place. There were so many of them that the walls looked quite black, and something like a black crepe fringe was hanging from the ceiling. Victor Borisovich shrugged his shoulders and closed the door. He caught sight of the sheet of paper by the coaming. A vague suspicion, something like the shadow of an idea, passed through his mind. For some minutes he stood lost in thought.

'Nonsense,' he said at last, and returned to the control panel.

It was becoming darker in the chart-room. Dense clouds of flies circled under the blue lighting tubes on the ceiling. Victor Borisovich raised his watch to his eyes. One and a half hours had passed since the beginning of the biological attack. He looked at the dead fly lying on the control panel and felt sick. He closed his eyes for a moment. Why on earth had he squashed it! Poison or no poison, it was a nasty thing all the same. Through his half-closed eyelids he noticed that the tape wasn't moving evenly. He corrected it, then his eyes reverted unvoluntarily to the squashed fly. At first he thought that it had disappeared. But then he located it again. It was moving. The navigator studied it attentively and swallowed with disgust. He was soaked with perspiration. The remains of the fly were covered with tiny black midges which were crawling rapidly over the squashed belly of the dead fly. There were about thirty of them, and they all had wide-spread wings although they could not fly yet. They crawled in all directions on the bright polished surface of the control panel.

This went on for about ten minutes. The blue tape kept coming out of the computer and dropping to the floor in spirals. Big black flies were flying around it. The navigator leaned forward and watched the dead fly with bated breath. To be more exact he was watching what had once been a dead fly. Looking closely at the fly's black leg, he noticed that it was covered with tiny pores, and from each pore the head of a microscopic fly was protruding. 'So that's why they multiply so rapidly,' thought Victor Borisovich. 'They simply come out of each other. Every cell has an embryo inside it. This fly cannot be killed, hundreds of replicas of itself come back to life.

The tiny flies were now crawling over the control panel, the buttons and verniers, and over the transparent plastic of the apparatus. There were quite a number of them already and some were even attempting to fly. A fine black powder was all that remained of the dead fly, and the navigator brushed it off the control panel in the same way that people brush away tobacco ash.

Through the ear-phones Victor Borisovich could hear Toomer's voice.

'The navigator is airing the chart-room,' he was saying.

Four men wearing shiny silicate suits and silvery helmets entered the chart-room.

'Why have you opened the door, Victor Borisovich?' asked the captain.

'The door?' Victor Borisovich turned round and looked at the door in surprise. 'I didn't open it.'

'But it was open,' said the captain.

Victor Borisovich shrugged his shoulders. The black midges, crawling out of the dead fly, were still before his eyes.

'I did not open the door,' he repeated.

He glanced at the door once more. Again he noticed the sheet of paper lying near the coaming and again a vague conjecture passed through his mind.

Lidin said impatiently:

'We had better decide what we are to do next.'

'The navigator doesn't know anything yet,' said the captain. 'Comrade Malyshev, repeat your conclusions once more, please.'

Malyshev cleared his throat.

'The equipment you've got is in poor condition,' he said, 'the microtome, for instance, seems to have been completely neglected ...'

He paused and Lidin could be heard giving instructions to somebody, probably Toomer: '... Take an alcohol cylinder and go round sprinkling them with alcohol. Then set fire to them ...'

'I'll try to be brief,' began Malyshev. 'The results of the chemical tests show that the composition of these flies is rather unusual; oxygen and nitrogen together with very small quantities of calcium, hydrogen and carbon. From this we can deduce that the flies represent some unknown, non-albuminous form of life. If so, then there is hardly any danger of their spreading infection, and then, of course, it is a discovery of primary importance. I want to lay particular stress on this last fact, as Comrade Lidin's only thought is how to destroy them. That is an erroneous approach to the problem.'

'If only we could get hold of some spiders,' said Lidin dreamily ... 'Some good old garden-spiders ...'

'We know nothing about them yet,' went on Malyshev. 'Neither what they feed on, nor how they multiply. But I think there is every reason to suppose that ...'

'I don't understand one thing,' interrupted Toomer. 'I killed dozens of them, squashed them with my feet, but I can't find a single dead fly.'

'Don't waste your time looking for one,' said the navigator. 'It's absolutely useless.'

'Why?'

Victor Borisovich noticed that the door had again opened slightly. The piece of paper fluttered as if it were trying to jump over the coaming, and fell back helplessly on the floor.

'I'll tell you all about it later,' he said. 'Later, when everything is over.'

Victor Borisovich went to the door, closed it, and returned to the table. The captain tapped the table slightly with his hand.

'Attention!' he snapped. 'I have decided to clear the ship of flies.'

'How?'

'We shall put on space-suits, raise the pressure inside the ship by using our reserve of liquid hydrogen, and open the hatches ...'

'Good Heavens!' muttered the navigator.

'. . . We shall let space into our ship, and then all this rubbish will be thrown out by the force of the compressed hydrogen.'

'Not a bad idea,' said Lidin.

Toomer dropped into an armchair and stretched out his legs.

'But we won't get rid of the spores like that,' he said.

'I think there are no more spores left on the ship,' complained Malyshev. 'They have all developed into flies.'

'We shall get rid of these creatures at last,' said Lidin, 'of these damned, nasty, devilish ...'

'I say,' interrupted Victor Borisovich, 'I think I have it at last.'

He went over to the door, stopped and touched the sheet of paper that lay by the coaming.

'What is it?' asked Toomer.

'Right,' said Stankevich, 'we shall go and fetch the vacuum suits. Lidin, you will help Malyshev with his suit.'

'All the flies will get frozen to death,' chuckled Lidin. He was terribly anxious for the flies to be frozen.

Victor Borisovich looked around him. All the walls were black. Black velvety festoons were hanging from the ceiling. The floor was covered with dry rustling pulp. It was getting dark – swarms of flies had clustered on the lighting tubes.

'Look here,' said Victor Borisovich, 'do you know why the door opens by itself?'

'What door, navigator?' asked the captain impatiently.

'Which door?' asked Toomer.

'This one, the one that leads into the corridor. It isn't opening any more now.'

'Well, what of it?'

'You see,' said Victor Borisovich hurriedly, 'the door opens outwards. If the pressure in the corridor drops, then the higher pressure in the chart-room pushes the door open. It's quite simple. But now there isn't any excess of pressure.'

'I don't understand you at all,' said the captain.

'It's all these flies' doing,' said Victor Borisovich.

'What has it got to do with flies?'

'The flies gobble up air. That's how they put on weight. They feed on air, on oxygen and nitrogen.'

The biologist mumbled something inarticulate, while the captain at once turned to look at the readings of the circulation system apparatus. Everyone was silent for several minutes. At last the captain announced:

'The apparatus shows that something like one

hundredweight of liquid oxygen has been spent during the last two hours.'

'How wonderful!' exclaimed Malyshev.

'The creatures!' said Lidin. 'The damned creatures!'

'I told you they were just eight-legged flies,' said Toomer. 'What else can one expect of them?'

'Logically speaking,' said the biologist, 'an atmosphere containing hydrogen ought to be fatal for them.'

'So much the better,' said the captain. 'Now, Lidin, you help Comrade Malyshev with his space-suit. Toomer, switch off the circulation system. Navigator, prepare the ship for vacuum and super-low temperature treatment. Report in ten minutes' time.'

Victor Borisovich walked towards the door reflecting on what would happen if a couple of flies were to get to Earth. One could not treat the Earth with vacuum and super-low temperatures.

He sighed, opened the door and charged head first into the black hole, scantily lit by a reddish glow.

They put on their vacuum suits directly on top of the protective suits. Then they made their way back to the chart-room through the long gloomy tunnel with black walls which once used to be the corridor. The walls of the tunnel were undulating slowly.

They entered the chart-room. Here, too, everything looked dark and unfamiliar.

'How's the circulation system, Toomer?' inquired the captain.

'Switched off.'

'And the hatches, navigator?'

'All opened, except the outside ones.'

'Lidin, have you checked the condition of the vacuum suits?'

'Yes, Comrade Captain.'

'Let us begin then,' said the captain.

Victor Borisovich looked at the manometer. Pressure inside the spaceship had fallen by thirty millimetres, although Toomer had switched the circulation system off only a few minutes before. The flies were sucking up the air and multiplying at a tremendous rate. The captain switched on the hydrogen supply. The manometer needle stopped, and then began to move slowly in the opposite direction. One atmosphere... One and a half... Two...

'Are there any flies in your space-suits?' inquired the captain.

'None that we know of,' replied Lidin.

There was silence again. They could hear nothing except one another's breathing coming through the earphones. Then somebody sneezed; it must have been Toomer.

'God bless you!' said Malyshev politely.

No one answered. Five atmospheres. The black pulp on the walls began to move heavily. 'So, there!' said Lidin maliciously. Six atmospheres.

'Stand by,' ordered the captain.

Victor Borisovich braced himself and caught hold of Malyshev's belt. Malyshev held on to Lidin and Lidin to the chair on which Toomer was sitting. The captain whisked a swarm of flies from the control-panel and pressed a button. Immediately four hatches that led to the freight compartment opened simultaneously.

Victor Borisovich felt a sudden jerk that shook him from head to foot. Somebody gasped. Under a pressure of six atmospheres the air-hydrogen mixture rushed through the hatches into space. A black blizzard whirled in the chart-room. And then it became light. Dazzlingly light. The chart-room was the same clean and sterile chart-room once more. Only some hoar-frost that sparkled in the blue light of the tubes, remained on the walls, and by the coaming there was nothing left but a slight film of dust.

'How nice it is!' said an unfamiliar hoarse voice.

'Attention,' said the captain, 'second stage!'

After that there was the third stage, then the fourth and

the fifth. Five times the ship was filled with compressed hydrogen, and five times whirls of compressed gas washed out every corner, every nook and cranny of the ship. The grey film of dust in front of the coaming disappeared, and so did the hoar-frost on the walls. Then the spaceship was filled with hydrogen for the sixth time. The captain switched on the dust catchers to their full capacity, and only after that had been done was air supplied to the ship.

'Well, that's all,' said Stankevich. 'For the present at least.'

He was the first to pull off his heavy space helmet.

'Maybe we dreamed it all?' said Lidin pensively.

'What a nice dream to have,' said Toomer.

Victor Borisovich was helping Malyshev to take off his spacesuit. When he pulled the ribbed sleeve down over the biologist's right hand, the captain suddenly said:

'And what have you got there, Comrade Malyshev?'

Malyshev was holding a small plastic box shaped like a spectacle case. He quickly hid his hand behind his back.

'Nothing in particular,' said the biologist, frowning.

'Comrade Malyshev!' said the captain in an icy tone.

'What, Comrade Stankevich?' returned the biologist innocently.

'Hand me that object immediately.'

'Good gracious,' exclaimed Victor Borisovich, 'he's got some flies there!'

'Well, and what of it?' said the biologist.

Lidin turned pale, then flushed.

'Destroy them at once,' he hissed. 'Throw them into the reactor immediately!'

'Take it easy, air engineer,' said Victor Borisovich.

Malyshev stepped out of his space-suit and put the box into his pocket. He raised his eyebrows and said:

'I am ashamed of you, comrades.'

This infuriated Lidin. 'Just listen to him, he is ashamed of us!' he cried.

'Yes, I am. I understand that it has all been rather sudden and... and frightening, but...'

'But can't you imagine what would happen if a single fly were to get into the Earth's atmosphere?'

'Do you know how they multiply?' asked the navigator.

'Yes, I know. I have seen it. This is quite ridiculous.' Malyshev stepped over his space-suit and settled down into an armchair. 'Listen to me for a minute. Life in Space may sometimes be inimical to life on Earth, that's true enough and it would be silly to deny it. But had there been the smallest chance of the flies threatening the life or health of mankind, I would be the first to demand that the spaceship be removed as far from Earth as possible and destroyed. But the flies aren't dangerous. Non-albuminous life cannot affect our form of life in the least. I am surprised at your ignorance and your nervousness.'

'The slightest carelessness,' persisted Lidin, 'and they will propagate themselves all over the Earth and eat up the whole atmosphere.'

Malyshev snapped his fingers contemptuously.

'If they propagate over the planet, I take it upon myself within two days to breed twenty-two kinds of nitro-oxygen viruses that will do away with the flies, their spores and twenty generations of offspring. Incidentally, we tried Lethal, Buxil, Petronal and other disinsectors, but I am sure that the best weapon against these flies would be ordinary spittle, as Toomer said in jest.'

Toomer burst out laughing.

'Damned if I understand a thing,' grumbled Stankevich.

'Well, I don't actually mean spit, but just plain water. Aqua distillata. I am quite positive about it.'

Malyshev gave a triumphant stare at the spacemen. Nobody said a word.

'Have you realized yet how extremely lucky we are?' he asked.

'No,' said Stankevich, 'not yet.'

'No? Well, let me explain once more. In the first instance we have at our disposal (he tapped his pocket) the most unique specimen of non-albuminous life. Up till now non-albuminous life could be reproduced only artificially. Do you understand that? Well, I'm glad to hear it. Secondly, try to picture to yourselves a plant which has neither machinery nor boilers. Instead, there is a giant insectarium where milliards of flies multiply and develop at incredible speed. The only necessary raw material is air. Hundreds of tons of first quality cellulose produced per day. And that means paper, fabrics, coating ... And all you have to say is "throw them into the reactor!" ...'

The biologist finished his speech, took out the plastic box and held it to his ear.

'Humming,' he announced. 'Unique creatures, extremely rare.'

He suddenly stopped and looked around in confusion.

'My snail,' he cried, and rushed out of the chart-room.

The spacemen looked at one another.

'Biology is the most important science, air engineer,' said Toomer. 'You ought to know that.'

'I am quite content with what I know of non-albuminous life,' said Lidin with disgust.

The captain rose to go.

'All's well that ends well,' he said without looking at Toomer. 'And if any of you ever start babbling about dangers from space ... Who's on watch?'

'Good heavens!' Victor Borisovich thought 'my watch isn't over yet! Can it be true that only three hours have passed?'

At the end of his watch, he dropped in to have a talk with Malyshev. The biologist was still mourning over the remnants of his glass tank. During the vacuum cleaning the pressure inside the ship had torn both the tank and the giant snail to pieces, and now the dried up shreds of the slug's body were hanging from the ceiling.

'It was such a rare specimen!' complained Malyshev.

'Never mind,' said the navigator, 'now you have got the flies instead. And next time I return from Titan, I shall bring you another slug. Let's go to the medical department and you can show me what's wrong with the microtome. You see, we never had a chance to use it before.'

Arkady Strugatsky

WANDERERS AND TRAVELLERS

THE water beneath the surface was not very cold and yet I felt chilled. I had been sitting at the bottom of the lake under the steep bank for more than an hour, carefully turning my head from side to side and peering into the green-coloured shadows. One had to sit very still because septopods are sensitive and mistrustful animals that can easily be frightened away by the slightest sound or abrupt movement, and then they would disappear and come back only at night – when it was better not to have anything to do with them.

An eel wriggled under my feet, and a pompous striped perch swam to and fro. Each time it passed, it stopped to stare at me with its round vacant eyes. When it left, a shoal of small silvery fish found a feeding-ground above my head. My shoulders and knees had become quite numb with cold and I was beginning to worry lest Masha should get tired of waiting for me and would dive into the water to my rescue. She would be waiting for me, sitting right at the edge of the water, worried and ready to start searching. I could picture her so clearly that I had almost made up my mind to get out; it was then that a septopod appeared from behind some water-plants only twenty paces away.

The septopod was rather a big specimen. It appeared all of a sudden, as noiselessly as a ghost, with its grey body thrusting forward. Its whitish mantle was throbbing in a soft, almost feeble manner, sucking in and throwing out water, and the septopod itself was slightly swaying from side to side as it went. Its arms, very much like the tattered ends of an old grey rag, were dragging behind it, while the narrow chink of its lustreless eye, half covered by the eyelid, shone wanly in the dim light. It swam slowly, as they usually do in the daytime, as if it were in a trance. I had no idea where it was going, or why. No doubt it was prompted by some dark and primitive urge such as guides the movements of amoebae.

I raised my marking rifle slowly and aimed at the septopod's inflated back. The little silvery fishes rushed aside and disappeared. It seemed to me that the eyelid covering the animal's eye moved. I pulled the trigger and immediately pushed off the ground to escape the caustic sepia. When I looked again, the septopod was nowhere to be seen, while a dense bluish-black inky fluid was dissolving in the water at the bottom of the lake. I surfaced and swam to the shore.

It was a hot fine day. A thin white mist hung over the lake and the sky was clear and blue. A few grey clouds were building up behind the woods.

A stranger was sitting on the grass in front of our tent. He wore brightly-coloured bathing trunks and a band around his forehead. He was sun-tanned and gave the impression of a very strong man, as if there were not muscles but strong ropes beneath his skin. Standing in front of him, in a blue bathing suit, was my daughter. My long-legged Masha, with her hair hanging down over her thin shoulders.

No, she wasn't waiting wistfully by the water for her father as I had pictured. She was chattering away with this wiry stranger, gesticulating and evidently explaining something to him. For a moment I felt hurt that she took no notice of my reappearance.

But the stranger had noticed me. He turned his head quickly and studied me attentively, then smiled and waved his hand. Masha turned round and shouted joyfully: 'Ah, here you are at last!'

I climbed out onto the grass, removed the diving-mask and wiped my face. The stranger continued to examine me with a smile on his face.

'How many have you marked?' asked Masha in a business-like manner. 'Only one,' I answered, my jaws still stiff with cold.

'Bad luck,' said Masha. She helped me to take off the aquastat and I stretched out on the grass.

'Yesterday he marked two septopods,' explained Masha, 'and four the day before yesterday. If it goes on like that, we shall have to move on to another lake.' She took a towel and began to rub me down. 'You look like a frozen goose,' she said laughingly. 'And this is Leonid Andreevich Gorbovsky. He is an astro-archaeologist. Leonid Andreevich, meet my father, Stanislav Ivanovich.'

Leonid Andreevich nodded.

'Feeling cold?' he asked. 'It's nice here – green grass, sunshine ...'

'He'll soon be all right,' said Masha, rubbing me with all her might. 'He's generally a cheerful fellow; it's just that he gets so cold in the water ...'

She must have been telling the man a lot of things about me and was now anxious to save my face. Let her, I thought. I had no time to trouble about it myself – I was busy trying to get warm again.

'Masha and I were rather worried about you down there,' said Gorbovsky. 'We even wanted to dive after you, only I don't know how. I suppose you can't imagine a man whose job has got nothing to do with diving and who has never dived in his life.' He had been lying on his back and now turned on his side, propping up his head with his hand. 'I fly away tomorrow,' he said confidentially. 'God knows when I shall be lying by a lake again and if I shall ever have the chance of diving with an aquastat ...'

'Go ahead then, try,' I offered.

He examined the aquastat carefully and touched it with his free hand.

'Sure,' he said, and rolled over onto his back. He put his hands under his head and lay there looking at me from beneath his thin eyelashes. There was something very prepossessing about him. I can't tell what exactly, but there it was. Maybe it was his eyes – so trusting and a little sad. Or maybe it was his ear that was sticking out from beneath the head-band in such a funny way. Having stared at me to his heart's content, he turned his gaze upon a blue dragon-fly that was balancing on a blade of grass.

He addressed it gently: 'Little dragon-fly, aren't you a beauty! So blue ... so transparent ... Sitting there quietly waiting for someone to gobble up ...' He stretched out his hand, but the dragon-fly took off and flew over to the rushes. Gorbovsky followed it with his eyes, then lay back again on the grass.

'How complex everything is, my friends,' he said meditatively, and Masha immediately sat down ready to listen, her eyes open wide. 'Just take this dragon-fly, for instance. So perfect, so graceful, and so content with everything! It gobbles up a fly, produces some offspring and then it is ready to die. Everything is simple, rational and elegant. No spiritual confusion, no love troubles, no self-consciousness, no aim in life ...'

'It's only a machine,' said Masha suddenly, 'a dull cybernetic machine!'

Well, wasn't she a bright child after all? I almost burst out laughing, but just managed to check myself in time – and only sniggered. Masha looked at me disapprovingly.

'Yes, it's dull,' agreed Gorbovsky. 'But just imagine, comrades, a giant dragon-fly with a wing-span of about seven metres, coloured a poisonous yellow-green with red stripes, and with foul black slime dripping from its jaws ...'

He raised his eyebrows and looked at us curiously. 'Well, I see that you have got quite a clear mental picture of it. Though I was armed, I remember running away from them like mad . . . Do you think they've got anything in common, these two dragon-flies?'

'The green one is from another planet, I suppose,' I asked.

'Yes, of course.'

'From Pandora?'

'Exactly.'

'You want to know what they've got in common?'

'Yes.'

'Well, it's clear enough,' said I. 'Their information handling processes are at the same stage of development. A reaction ruled by instinct.'

'Words,' he sighed. 'No offence meant, but those are just mere words. They don't help me in the least. My task is to find some traces of Reason in the universe, and I am still not clear myself as to what Reason is. I am continually being told about different stages of information handling processes. I know that this dragon-fly and myself are at different stages, but I know it only by intuition. For instance, I find a termite-mound. How am I to know whether it has been constructed by an intelligent mind or not? On Leonida they found some buildings with neither windows nor doors. Are they the fruit of an intelligent mind? What am I to hunt for? Ruins? Inscriptions? Or rusty nails perhaps? What do I know of the traces these other creatures leave behind them? Suppose their sole aim in life is to destroy atmosphere wherever they encounter it ... who knows? Or to build rings around the planets ... or to hybridise life ... or to create new life? For all I know, this dragon-fly might be a cybernetic machine that had the power of self-reproduction built into it many years ago. I am not speaking now of the bearers of Reason themselves. One could pass a dozen times by some nasty slippery monster wallowing in the dirt without taking any notice of it, while the monster keeps staring at you all the time with its round yellow eyes – and thinking: How very interesting! It must be a new kind. I'll come back here some day with an expedition and try to catch one ...'

He covered his eyes with his hand and started humming a tune. Masha sat staring at him and waiting for him to go on. I waited too, and thought sympathetically how difficult it is to work on a problem that has not been clearly defined. To keep on wandering in the darkness, finding no pleasure in one's job. I've heard about these astro-archaeologists. No one takes them seriously.

'And yet there is Reason in the Universe,' Gorbovsky suddenly said. 'There's no doubt about it. But it's quite different from what we expect it to be, and we just go on looking for it in the wrong place without having a definite idea of what we are looking for ...'

'That's true,' I thought. 'No definite idea, the wrong place ... The whole thing is extremely childish. Trying to find traces of ideas that once floated in the air.'

'Take, for instance, the Voice of Empty Space,' he continued. 'Have you ever heard about it? Probably not. Some fifty years ago they used to write a lot on the subject, but then they gave it up – couldn't discover anything. We've still got some "scientists" who, owing to their own laziness or poor education, advocate a sort of cheap anthropocentrism. Somewhere they have picked up the idea that Man is omnipotent, and they cannot allow themselves to admit that he is unable to solve the problem of the Voice. So they think it best to say that there isn't any Voice at all ...'

'But what is it, "the Voice of Empty Space"?' asked Masha in a low voice.

'It's rather a curious phenomenon observed in some parts of the cosmos. If you set your on-board wireless for automatic tuning, sooner or later you will hear a calm indifferent voice that keeps repeating one and the same sentence in an unknown tongue. For many years they've been picking it up and many people have heard it, but they don't like to speak of it. It's not a very pleasant experience, you see. Imagine yourself on board a spaceship, alone on watch somewhere inconceivably far from Earth. The ether is free so there are no disturbances, only a faint rustling. And suddenly there is the Voice. Everyone else is asleep, and you are all alone in Space with it. It's really frightening, enough to make your flesh creep. Some recordings of the Voice have been made. Many scientists have tried to decipher it, and some still haven't given up, but to my mind they are just wasting their time. There are some other unsolved problems too, besides the Voice. Spacemen could tell you many an interesting story, but they don't like to blab ...' He stopped and added with a sort of sad persistence: 'It should be understood that it's no simple matter. We don't even know what to expect. We could meet them any moment, face to face. And, you know, they may turn out to be much superior to us. A great deal is said about various collisions and conflicts, about a different understanding of what is good and human, but that isn't what I fear. What I am afraid of is an unprecedented humiliation of mankind. If that were to happen, it would be a great emotional shock. We are used to being so proud of ourselves. We have created such a wonderful world, we know so much, we have broken out into the Great Universe which we are discovering and investigating as if it were something quite new, while for them the Universe is their native home. They have been living there for millions of years just as we have on Earth and they merely wonder about us: "Where have these strange creatures arrived from?"'

He stopped abruptly and rose to his feet, listening to something. I started.

'It's thunder,' said Masha quietly. She was staring at him open-mouthed. 'It's thunder,' she repeated, 'we'll have a thunderstorm soon ...'

Still he kept listening, searching the sky attentively with his eyes.

'No, it isn't thunder,' he said at last, and sat down. 'It's a liner. Can't you see it over there?'

A bright strip of light flashed through the dark clouds and disappeared. A faint noise of thunder was heard.

'Now I've got to sit here and wait,' he said vaguely.

He looked at me pleasantly and there was sadness and tense expectation in his eyes. Then it all disappeared, he relaxed and his eyes had the same trusting look in them again.

'And what are you working on, Stanislav Ivanovich?' he asked.

I realized that he wanted to change the subject and began telling him about the septopods. I told him that these animals belong to the dibranchia sub class in the cephalopod molluscs group, and represent a special and previously unknown tribe of the octopus order. They have the following distinctive features: a reduced third left arm conjugate to the third right hectocodyledonal arm, three rows of suckers on each arm, an extremely powerful venous heart and no coelom whatsoever. I explained that they also have a highly developed and concentrated nervous system that distinguishes the septopods from all other representatives of the cephalopod group. There are some additional minor peculiarities not worth mentioning. The septopods were discovered quite recently when some individuals appeared on the east and south-east coast of Asia. A year later they were found in the lower reaches of the Mekong, the Yangtze, the Hwang Ho and the Amur, and in some small lakes situated at a considerable distance from the coast, as, for instance, in this lake. This is very striking, because cephalopods cannot live without salt and therefore they even tend to avoid arctic waters with their low salinity. And they almost never come out onto dry land. But septopods feel quite at home in fresh water bodies such as this lake and are not afraid to come out on to the banks. They get into boats and climb on to bridges, and quite recently two of them were found in a wood some thirty kilometres from here...

Masha wasn't listening. She had heard it all a dozen times before. She went to the tent and came back carrying our radio. She switched on the automatic tuner and was evidently trying to pick up the Voice.

Gorbovsky, however, was particularly interested.

'And were those two specimens alive?' he asked.

'No, they were found dead. You see, this is a forest reserve, and the septopods had been trampled and half-eaten by wild boars. But they had been alive thirty kilometres away from the lake. Their mantle cavity was full of wet water plants. Probably the septopods preserve water for their land marches in this way. They must have been moving inland from these lakes in a southerly direction. It should be noted that all the captured individuals have been adult males. Not a single female or young one. Probably they can neither live in fresh water nor come out on land.

'All this is extremely interesting,' I went on, 'for as a rule sea-animals only change their mode of life as sharply as this during the period of reproduction. Then their propagation instinct urges them to move to unknown places. But with septopods this is absolutely out of the question. They are guided by some other instinct, more ancient and powerful. We are mainly concerned now with the problem of their migrations.

'That's why I keep sitting in this lake for ten hours a day. Today I marked one. If I am lucky, I shall mark a couple more before it gets dark. At night they become very aggressive and attack anything that tries to approach them, even humans. But that's only at night.'

Masha had now turned the wireless up to its full capacity and was enjoying the din.

'Turn it down a little, Masha,' I asked.

She complied.

'So you mark them,' said Gorbovsky. 'How odd! And with what, may I ask?'

'With supersonic generators,' I said pulling the magazine out of the marking rifle and handing him an ampule. 'We mark them with these "bullets". Inside the "bullets" there is a generator that can be heard in the water at a distance of some twenty or thirty kilometres.'

He took the ampule and examined it carefully. His face turned old and sad.

'Clever,' he muttered, 'very clever, and so simple ...'

He went on turning it round in his fingers, then put it on the grass in front of me and got to his feet. He walked slowly and uncertainly over to his clothes, picked up his trousers and then stood still, holding them absently in his hands.

I watched him with some anxiety. Masha was holding the marking gun eager to explain how it worked, and she was watching Gorbovsky too, the corners of her mouth drooping mournfully. She is a sensitive child, and I have noticed several times that her face is apt to adopt the same expression as that of someone she is watching.

Then, speaking in a low voice filled with irony, Gorbovsky said:

'It's really quite funny, to tell the truth ... Such a close analogy! For centuries they used to sit in the depths and now they have risen to the surface and come out into an unknown and hostile world ... What urges them on? An ancient dark instinct, you say? Or a method of handling information that has reached the stage of extreme curiosity? It certainly would have been better for the creatures to stay at home in the salty water, but something induces them to venture onto dry land ...'

He roused himself and started pulling on his long old-fashioned trousers, hopping awkwardly on one leg.

'Tell me, Stanislav Ivanovich, these septopods are not just primitive cephalopods, are they?'

'Certainly not,' I answered.

But he wasn't listening. He had turned towards the wireless and was staring at it. Powerful but somewhat disharmonious signals, like the disturbances caused by an X-ray installation, were coming from it. Masha put down the marking rifle.

'6.08,' she said, looking perplexed. 'It must be a service station.'

Gorbovsky listened to the signals with closed eyes and with his head inclined a little to one side.

'No,' he said at last, 'it's not a service station. It's me.'

'What?'

'Yes, it's me who is signalling, me, Leonid Andreevich Gorbovsky.'

'What for?'

He laughed a little. It was a sad laugh.

'Ask me another,' he said. 'I should like to know that myself.' He pulled on his shirt. 'Why, on returning from their regular cruise number EN 101 – EN 2657, have three pilots and their spaceship become the source of radio waves with a length of 6.083 metres?'

We remained silent. He stopped for a moment, and bent down to buckle his sandals.

'We have been examined by doctors. We have been examined by physicists.' He rose and brushed the sand and pieces of grass from his trousers. 'And they all came to the conclusion that it was impossible. One could have laughed oneself into a fit at their puzzled faces. But as for us, we were really past laughing. Tolya Obozov refused to take his holiday and went to Pandora. He said he preferred to emit signals as far from Earth as possible. Valkenstein went to work at a submarine station. Only I remained here, wandering around and signalling. And all the time I expect something to happen. I don't know exactly what, but it frightens me. I am full of anticipation and fear at one and the same time. Do you follow me?'

'I don't know,' I said dubiously, and looked at Masha out of the corner of my eye.

'You are right,' he said catching the hint. He took the wireless out of Masha's hands and raised it to his ear.

'Nobody knows. It's been going on for a month now without interruption and the signals don't seem to get any weaker. "Wha ... whee ... wha ... whee" – like that, day and night. No matter whether we are happy or sad, hungry or well fed, or working or just loafing about. "Wha ... whee ..." all the time. Tariel is emitting less, however. "Tariel" is my spaceship. It has been laid up for the present. Just to be on the safe side. Its signals are jamming some control signals directed to Venus, and this annoys the operators over there; they keep sending inquiries. Tomorrow I shall take it away somewhere farther away ...' He drew himself to his feet and slapped his sides with his hands. 'Well, it's time I was going. Good-bye! I wish you luck. Good-bye, Mashenka! Don't start racking your young brains over what I've been saying. It's much too complicated for you.'

He waved his hand, nodded and walked away. He looked very long-legged and awkward. When he was passing our tent, he stopped for a moment and said:

'You should be more considerate with those septopods, you know. This marking of yours might be the cause of some serious trouble for the creatures ...'

He left. I lay in the grass on my stomach for a while, then looked at Masha. She was following Gorbovsky with her eyes. It was clear that Leonid Andreevich had produced a deep impression on her. But not on me. I wasn't in the least troubled by his considerations about the bearers of Universal Reason being much superior to us. Let them be. To my mind the more superior they proved to be, the less chances there were of our getting in their way. We would be like the small fry that easily swim through the large meshes of a fishing-net. As to pride, humiliation, emotional shock ... Probably we would get over that, somehow. I am sure I would. The fact that we are discovering and studying a Universe which has long been known and inhabited by them makes no difference. We haven't made ourselves at home there yet! They are still only a part of nature for us to discover and investigate, no matter how superior to us they might be ... They are outsiders, and that's that.

Although, let's face it, if I were to be marked the way I mark the septopods ...

I looked at my watch and sat up. It was time to get down to work again. I copied down the number of the last ampule, checked the aquastat, then went over to the tent where I picked up the supersonic locater and put it into the pocket of my bathing trunks.

'Give me a hand, Masha,' I said, and started pulling on the aquastat.

Masha was still sitting in front of the wireless and listening to the unfading 'wha ... whee ...' She came over and helped me with the aquastat, and we both stepped into the water. I switched on the locater under the water. The signals started sounding – my marked septopods were wandering dreamily about the lake. I exchanged a significant look with Masha and launched out. Masha spat out some water, brushed back the wet hair from her forehead and said:

'Still, there must be a difference between a spaceship and a slippery bag of wet seaweed ...'

I told her to wait on shore, and submerged. No, if I were Gorbovsky, I shouldn't be so nervous. It is not to be taken seriously, and the same with all that astro-archaeological nonsense of his. Traces of ideas ... Emotional shock ... There won't be any shock. Most likely we won't even notice one another's existence. What do they care about us, after all?

G. Gor

THE BOY

I

HERMAN IVANOVICH walked into the classroom carrying a pile of our copy-books. Taking one of them he turned to us and said in his usual quiet, tired voice:

'If Gromov doesn't mind I'll read his homework out loud. I think you will find it interesting.'

He began to read. He read magnificently and we felt at once that the story was about something very strange and extraordinary. About a boy lost in the cold, boundless universe.

The Boy had been born along the way, among the stars, and the spaceship, a copy in miniature of the planet left behind, to which the grown-ups, his mother and father and companions failed to get used in the course of a decade, was to him seomething ordinary and habitual like our schoolyard was to us.

Somewhere in the infiniteness of the universe they had left far behind the dense evergreen forests, blue rivers, houses full of merriment and noise and long roads. The Boy could watch all this on the screen, but to him it was all bits of dreams. Perhaps all this had never really existed . . .?

His companions tried very hard and insistently to prove to the Boy that all this had really existed, but it was the dreamer – the musician, who managed to do this better than anyone else. Listening to his music the Boy could see the forests and rivers, the houses and roads of the distant planet that the expedition had left, long before he was born. It made him want to stretch out his hands and touch this world shimmering on the screen before him which was so unlike the life on the spaceship, but even if his hands could have stretched for millions of kilometres, they would not have reached the forests and rivers, houses and roads – they were all that far away.

But all this really existed. The music said so. And it was proved by the screen and knowledge: the Boy did not just live on the spaceship – he studied too.

Everyone taught the Boy – his parents and the rest of the grown-ups. Even the commander of the ship, who was always busy with something, found time to teach him. The memory machines carefully preserved the knowledge of the past and passed it on fully to the Boy. But the Boy often thought that he would have given all this knowledge in exchange for only one hour in the forest on the bank of the swift-running river. It was music that told him of the forest and the river. The musician also pined for the home he had left behind and he made no effort to hide his longing. He had the right to show his feelings as he was a musician and a dreamer. His grief did not interfere with the life and work of his companions – it even helped them.

The Boy went on with his studies. He had no chums of his own age. Just as he had never seen real rivers and forests, the only children he had ever seen were on the screen. He had no one to play with except the little robot, an amusing toy made especially for him. But the robot was too serious and businesslike – so dull and monotonous.

The Boy often wondered what children were really like. He wanted to see them in his dreams, but he never did, not even once.

The Boy made inquiries of the grown-ups, who were always so kind and attentive to him, and of the machines that knew everything, but none could tell him anything sensible or convincing about children. Neither the grown-ups, nor machines, nor the screen. Not even the music. Perhaps the reason was that they didn't want to tell the Boy of their own childhood which had been spent not on a spaceship falling in a black, ice-cold abyss.

But the Boy very seldom thought of this abyss. The spaceship in itself was a whole world to him. And in this world there were prohibited corners, where the grown-ups did not allow the Boy to enter, each time putting him off with promises that he would be allowed to enter when he grew up.

When he grew up? These words frightened and brought joy to the Boy with their slightly strange and obscure meaning. On the ship he was the only one growing up. Everyone else had grown up back home on their planet long before they had left it. He alone was growing up and changing and everyone noticed this with a certain sadness as a sign of the implacable passing of time, more implacable here, on the spaceship, than back at home. The Boy was growing and changing, but he still had a long way to grow and change before he would become grown-up.

Where was the spaceship going, what for? The Boy instinctively felt that the grown-ups did not like to answer these questions. They were not prohibited, but there was a great deal that was not clear. The spaceship was to take the expedition to one of the planets near the Big Star, to find out if there were any reasoning creatures there. This was a subject for heated dispute. Part of the expedition considered that there must be and part were very much in doubt. The Boy was a bit doubtful himself. Perhaps this was because his father was among those who were doubtful. The Boy loved his father more than anyone else in the world, even more than he loved the musician, although he didn't know why he loved him so much. His father had a nervous face which jerked with a tic. But the Boy liked his face even though it had a tic.

Sometimes a strange brilliance appeared in his father's eyes, and the Boy knew that, unlike many others, his father could not and did not want to hide his yearning impatience to reach the planet near the Big Star as quickly as possible. The Boy forgave his father his impatience because he guessed at its cause. The Boy's father was a geologist and a great part of his life was passing away in idleness on the spaceship where he could not put his knowledge and effort to use. For many years now his father had been pining for the work he loved. The Boy's mother, who was an expert in forests and trees, had also spent years in tiresome waiting. Evidently on that planet she was hoping to find extraordinary large and thick forests full of strange trees which had been waiting for centuries to have someone come and give them names and determine their nature. It was quite possible that there were no reasoning creatures on that planet.

It was really amazing that nearly everything had already been named, and that, to give names to the unnamed, it was necessary to travel through millions and millions of kilometres and decades of years. The Boy lived among names and titles.

Among the living beings populating the spaceship he was the only one who was hardly in need of a name. Everyone just called him Boy, even his mother and father.

'Boy!' his companions would call out.

'Boy!' the toy-robot would say, as they played.

On the part of an inanimate object this was, of course, a somewhat familiar form of address. But the boy did not feel insulted. The robot could not answer for his words. He spoke according to a dictated programme.

'Boy!' the grown-ups would say, 'how did you spend your day?'

And their faces, he noticed, would brighten up and become more carefree. Now why was that? Who could tell? Perhaps it was because when they looked at the Boy they remembered themselves as he was now. Only the face of the ship's commander did not brighten up when he saw the Boy. He remained as stern and busy as ever. And the Boy understood and approved of his behaviour. The commander did not allow his thoughts to carry him back to the past and so make his life in the spaceship more easy. In sparing others he never spared himself and thoughts of the responsibility he carried never left him.

The commander would go off to his cabin, or to his instruments and assistants. The Boy would stay where some interest in some phenomena, some thing or someone had caught his fancy. He was always interested in something and was never at a loss for something to do.

'Boy!' his companions called out to him.

Things also called out to the Boy, even those things that could neither speak nor think.

And the Boy would answer.

2

Herman Ivanovich stopped reading and put down the copybook.

'What comes next?' someone asked.

'Next,' Herman Ivanovich answered, changing his voice back to its normal tone, becoming the old, worn and tired teacher we knew. 'Next there is nothing but a full stop. Let us hope that Gromov will some time finish the story. As it is, the story has no end.'

The Boy had disappeared. But there was Gromov, seated near the window, pretending that he had nothing whatsoever to do with the Boy. There was an expression of tense alertness on his face as if he expected us to play some dirty trick on him. But honestly, none of us had the slightest idea of doing any such thing. As far as that goes he had let himself down by writing that strange story for homework.

Gromov was the last person who should write about that Boy. Everyone knew he was the son of a well-known archaeologist, and that several years ago, his father had made some great discovery. He had discovered some puzzling things that had been the subject for a great deal of controversial dispute. Articles had appeared in the evening paper and several magazines, about Gromov's father finding traces of aliens from other planets. But for some reason the magazines had stopped writing about it just as they had stopped writing about the Snowman whom the newspapers had made such a fuss about at first. School gossip had it that it wasn't true – both about the aliens and the Snowman. Everyone had already begun to believe in the Snowman and so they were all sorry to part with him, of course.

None of the kids wanted to be in Gromov's shoes when all the magazines suddenly stopped writing about his father's archaeological findings. And when Gromov was around we tried not to talk on archaeological subjects as we understood that it wasn't his fault. Of course it wasn't Gromov's father's fault either that some reporter had been in a hurry to make such a fuss about something that was still a matter of dispute instead of waiting patiently until the scientists would settle the problem authoritatively.

Gromov took it hard. He always kept to himself and walked home alone and never invited any of the kids over to his place except me and Vlassov. But Vlassov was a quiet boy who was always stammering with shyness, and Gromov just couldn't help inviting me over as I lived in the house right opposite and had even broken a window in his apartment – but that was long before his father had made his discovery. Gromov was afraid that if he didn't invite me over I would think it was because of the broken window. The glass in that window cost a lot of money. It was a thick one, like in a shop window.

If you don't count Vlassov, who was so shy he was afraid to look around in a strange apartment, I was the only one in the class who knew the inside of Gromov's apartment well. It was a large old-fashioned flat. And it always had a strange smell about it which was impossible to place. There were several yellow and brown skulls up on top of a cupboard with figures written on them, and a little wooden idol on the wall, which stared at everyone with its transparent cruel-looking eyes made of obsidian – a volcanic glass, as Gromov had explained.

Neither Gromov nor his father ever invited me or Vlassov into the study. And every time I was in the apartment I looked at the study door with curiosity wondering what was behind it, thinking that there must be all kinds of rare things and probably even those that had been the cause of all those fierce arguments among the scientists. Deep down in my heart I was sorry that the reporters had stopped writing about the findings of Gromov's father. I don't know why, but for some reason I wanted Gromov's father to prove to his opponents that he was right. The kids said that I didn't stand up for the truth but for false pride and vanity because I was Gromov's friend. But that wasn't true. I valued the truth very much, but I wanted one thing: I wanted the truth to be something extraordinary and interesting. There are too many ordinary and uninteresting truths in this world as it is.

3

If anyone had asked me to describe Gromov's character or what he looked like I don't think I could have. He looked like any ordinary boy except for the grey lock of hair over his left ear. It had turned grey as soon as he was born, long before he learned to worry or be sad about anything. His grey lock of hair and glasses in greenish-coloured frames gave a serious and grown-up looking expression to his face. One of the kids had called him an academician, but the nickname hadn't stuck. Nothing seemed to stick to Gromov: neither dirt nor dust nor envy nor cruel words. In some ways he was like the Boy he had written about in his story.

It wasn't just because of his grey lock, but because he knew a great deal about a lot of things. None at school knew as much as Gromov did, although he was never at the top of the class. The thing was his knowledge had no connection whatsoever with the school programme. For instance he managed to know the exact size of the brain of the plesiosaurus which had become extinct millions of years ago. Even Ivan Stepanovich, the biology teacher, didn't know that. But we couldn't understand what sense there was in knowing things like that if they weren't included in the text books or school programme. Except for Herman Ivanovich the teachers didn't think much of this sort of knowledge. Of course it would have been stupid to think that they only valued the knowledge that could be found in the text books and school prgramme. They were just practically minded and understood that knowing how large the brain of a plesiosaurus was, could hardly be of use to Gromov in the future and that one had to acquire knowledge that could be used in everyday life. It could hardly be expected that he, or we, or you, would ever come face to face with a plesiosaurus.

Once I spoke straight out and said the same to Gromov. He looked at me mockingly, pulled a newspaper cutting out of his school bag, and handed it to us. We read it and our eyes nearly popped out of their sockets. The article stated that a few days ago a real live plesiosaurus had been discovered in one of the Scottish lakes.

During the biology lesson we showed the article to Ivan Stepanovich and for some reason he was embarrassed and even seemed displeased at the discovery. At the end of the lesson he said:

'That doesn't change a thing.'

Then, after thinking a moment, he said:

'But there is no loss either.'

His words were no less puzzling to us at the time than the discovery of the plesiosaurus.

But that's enough about the plesiosaurus. Everyone knows about it anyway. But Gromov knew a lot about things that there weren't the slightest mention of in our text books. He knew things about water that none of us did. And he knew things about ice that Vera Nikolaevna, our chemistry teacher, most likely knew nothing about. Once, at the chemistry lesson, he said that ice was not a solid as many people think it is.

'And what is it?' we were interested to know.

'Solids are bodies, the particles of which compose a regular structure, a crystal lattice.

The thought of glass, which is so hard you have to use a diamond cutter, struck me and I asked Gromov a perfidious question.

'What about glass,' I asked. 'Is it a solid?'

'No,' Gromov answered. 'Glass is a super-cooled liquid of high viscidity.'

Vera Nikolaevna didn't take part in the conversation. Where chemistry or physics was concerned it was better not to come up against Gromov. No one knew the source of his knowledge and it was difficult to check whether he was right or not.

When Gromov was silent he was just an ordinary schoolboy like the rest of us. But as soon as he opened his mouth he changed completely. He seemed to become bigger and cleverer than the rest of us, as if that was his real self, and he was keeping the fact under cover until the right time came.

He never hurried to answer any of the teacher's questions, as the top pupils usually did. On the contrary, he spoke very slowly as if he didn't know the right answer and was mutely asking the advice of someone inside of himself.

4

When I walked into the classroom, Gromov was in his seat near the window reading a book.

I said hello, and then, quite unintentionally, blurted out:

'What about the Boy? Are you going to write any more about him?'

I thought he'd pretend he hadn't heard, but he answered me, and rather willingly, at that.

'Herman Ivanovich has the copy book. I managed to get hold of more information.'

'But you thought that Boy up ... it's just a story ... a fantasy ...'

Gromov looked at me and answered with a question:

'Are you sure of that?'

'Aren't you sure of that?'

He grinned and uttered the words, the meaning of which I couldn't get to the bottom of, no matter how I tried.

'It doesn't matter in the least whether anyone is sure of it. The whole thing is much more complicated.'

After lessons were over Herman Ivanovich read us the continuation of the story. This time his reading was much worse.

The spaceship continued on its journey. The Boy was the happiest one on board because he had been born on the ship and knew about other things only from what he had been taught or told by his companions. Unlike them he had left no one behind on the home planet that he missed or pined for. Everyone he had ever known were all here, with him on the spaceship. His present and his past were here; as for what the future held, he could only guess. His future depended on the theory of probability and the unknown planet they were flying to. There was a great deal said about that planet aboard the ship. Everyone had his own ideas about what it was like. Some considered that it was inhabited by highly reasoning and civilized beings. Others argued that the time hadn't come for reasoning beings to inhabit the planet and that it was inhabited by pangolins. The Boy had his own hypothesis. He was certain that the planet was inhabited by children. Deep down in his heart he understood that this was impossible. But he wanted so much to see some children before he grew up and became old. The Boy never told anyone about his hypothesis. He was afraid of the cold and relentless logic of the grown-ups who would try to prove to him as they proved a theorem, that his dream was just a castle built on air, and could never come true.

In the course of many years of continous non-stop flight a certain life rhythm of its own had been established aboard the spaceship. This rhythm made life easier for all the members of the expedition so that they hardly thought of the fact that only the walls of the ship separated them from the cold and horrible emptiness of the universe.

The Boy learned that there was a name for this rhythm. It was called the trivialities of everyday life. Try as hard as he could he couldn't understand the real meaning of this word, although he always caught the meaning of other names and words at once. Perhaps the grown-ups had decided, as soon as they boarded the spaceship, never to think of the bottomless abyss, and then this rhythm had appeared which kept them from thinking alarming thoughts, just as sleep or work does.

There were representatives of nearly all the professions on board the spaceship. There was a philosopher too. He found sense for everything that happened around them and with the help of reasoning put everything in its right place.

Once he met the philosopher in the section of logical machines. He worked up the courage and asked him what the trivialities of life meant.

The philosopher smiled at the Boy tenderly.

'The trivialities of life,' he said, 'are a chain of habits that we really don't notice, as we don't notice the clothes that we wear. But if we take off our clothes and go out into the cold frost ...'

The philosophere suddenly went silent, remembering that he was not talking to a grown-up, but to a boy.

He smiled at him once again and walked off.

The Boy never repeated his question and tried not to think of it. He guessed that everyday trivialities existed only for grown-ups. That there were no such things for children and that there couldn't possibly be. Everything that the Boy saw was new and interesting to him, even the things that he had seen many, many times.

He saw how hard everybody worked, calculating, inventing or studying something. He visited the laboratories. Wherever he went everyone was glad to see him, especially in the laboratories where they experimented with the most complicated phenomena, particularly in the laboratory of sub-molecular biology. Perhaps this was because the scientists went so deep into the study of the 'unseen' and 'unknown', which they could approach only with the most complicated of instruments, and for hours lost contact with the surrounding world, and the Boy appeared to them as a messenger from that wonderful world.

In their off hours some of the participants of the expedition played chess. The Boy would look over the shoulder of one of the players and try to guess what the next move would be. The musician was the worst player of them all. He lost to everyone – to both the machines and his live partners. And he always took it very hard, but couldn't keep from playing. His continuous losses vexed the Boy terribly.

Having lost a game the musician would go off to his cabin to compose music. Once he beckoned to the Boy and led him into his cabin. He switched on the recorder so that the Boy could hear the new melody he had composed.

The Boy listened and the sounds poured out, ethereal and bright. He could hear bits of ice as they broke and shattered against each other, he could hear the song of water as it bubbled and murmured and then flowed on to thunder and beat against the rocky boulders it met along in its path.

And little by little the Boy could see the unknown planet they were flying to with its myriads of rivers and streams. The water sang a wonderful and amazing song.

And suddenly the Boy felt that the song was there but there were no ears to hear it or reason to understand it. The time for reasoning beings had not yet come to that planet ... The planet that the music was telling about.

And then a silence fell. They were both silent – the composer and the Boy. But a boy is a boy, and he could not keep silent for long.

'Please tell me,' he said.

'About what?'

'The same old thing,' the Boy pleaded quietly.

And the musician understood what the Boy was asking about and he began to tell him about the planet where he was born and where he had spent his youth. He was a good musician but a bad narrator and often got mixed up and stopped at places and repeated himself over and over again.

But besides the mountain paths and trees and the mountains with the lake at the top, the musician said, there was also something else that is called necessity. When the musician grew up he had to leave the paths and river and the mountain with the lake at its very top up among the blue clouds. An automobile as swift as lightning brought him to the city. It was all right in the city too. But in the city there was no mountain with a lake at the top. But the musician did not lose heart. By that time he already knew that life is composed of both gain and loss.

And for the first time the thought came to the Boy that the distance the spaceship had to cover could be measured not in time and space but by life time. And that was amazing ... The years were passing. And even if the musician ever managed to see his mountain again, it would be when he had become old and feeble.

There was only one very old man on the spaceship. He was the chief calculating technician, the expert who was in charge of the computers. Everyone knew he would never reach home again. He was too old for that.

The Boy examined the old man on the sly. There was

something in common between him and the old man. The old man was the oldest on the ship and the Boy was the youngest.

Did that man ever have a childhood? Possibly he did have. He couldn't have become old all at once. Whenever he came upon the Boy he exclaimed in amazement:

'However did you get here, Boy?'

The Boy understood that it was just his way of joking. But was there any sense in repeating the same thing over and over again? The Boy who had no past at all and the old man who had a past which held nearly as much as the memory machine, the keeper of data and facts. But the past kept silent from a feeling of dignity. The old man wasn't a memory machine ready to answer anyone at all no matter how foolish the question. And the past in the old man's memory was quite different from that in the memory of the information instruments. The machines remembered dates and facts, incidents and events. Besides all these facts and events that had taken place the old man remembered himself and other people as well.

It is strange, incidentally, that on the night when the abyss nearly swallowed up the spaceship, the Boy should have suddenly thought of the old man. But the story about the Abyss and the spaceship and the Boy will come later.

'And that's all for now,' Herman Ivanovich said with a strange note in his voice, which sounded both sad and glad, we couldn't tell which, and closed the copy-book. 'We shall look forward to the continuation.'

5

I felt as if something were missing. Gromov seemed to have been carried away by the memory machines and the old man and had wandered away from the main subject of the story.

Like the rest of the kids, I was expecting the Boy to do

some brave deed of daring or heroic act. But there didn't seem to be any heroic deed forthcoming. Everything in the story dragged along so ordinarily and so tiresomely slow, just as things do when you are getting ready for exams. And then, at the end, something did happen. But we didn't know what.

We did all sorts of calculating. We calculated as to how large the spaceship would have to be to hold all that was necessary for such a long journey. We kept on asking Gromov how many people were aboard, how many machines, what kind of energy was used on the ship – light energy, or atom energy or energy connected with the use of anti-gravitation forces? Whether the ship used the ordinary Einstein time or zero space, which science-fiction writers wrote about.

We had a lot of arguments about the theory of zero space. No one could make head or tail of it. Dorofeyev, our top pupil, said it was a phenomenon that no one understood anything about except the science-fiction writers. Then we had a go at Gromov. He said that we had to drop the idea of zero space because the Boy lived in quite a normal three dimensional world and that the ship moved at a speed somewhere near to the speed of light.

Some sort of communication – it wasn't the telephone, or telegraph, or radio or quantum communication, but clearly psychological, one might say, kept us in contact with the Boy who lived somewhere in the past or future in some unknown spot in the universe.

I had read somewhere that research in the field of communication had still a great distance to go. That the subject had not yet been probed to the full. Some scientists assert that there exists a so-called psi-field, the physical nature of which is not yet known. The spaceship Boy took on reality and became an everyday part of our life. To understand the atmosphere that surrounded the Boy we began to follow all the news that appeared in connection with science and engineering. We were all in a feverish state of activity. Leonid Starovertsev even started a card file and wrote down every new event in science discoveries and techniques on a separate card. He usually carried the cards around in his pockets, and, during lessons, he would pull them out, one by one, wrinkling up his near-sighted eyes, as he went over them. And what you couldn't find on those cards wasn't worth looking for! He had everything on them from super-new stars, nucleic acids, the automatic memory of birds at birth, the cleverness of dolphins, to the language of the ancient Mayans and community-mindedness of bees and ants that communicated with each other exclusively with the help of ultra-sound.

Starovertsev sat in front of me, and, peeking over his shoulder, I could add all this to my store of knowledge.

Once I asked Starovertsev if he had any notes on the Snowman.

'No, I've left that card open for future information,' he said.

'Why did you do that?' I asked.

'Because I'm waiting till science finds an answer to that controversial problem.'

Those cold laconic words of his made me feel bad. That meant that the card which should have had notes on Gromov's father's discoveries had also been left unfilled and was waiting for science to solve that controversial problem too.

6

Gromov occupied his usual seat near the window, and when I wanted to take a look at Gromov I pretended that I wanted to look out of the window. The window was big and wide and bright and looked out upon the street down below with its trees and people on the sidewalks. Across from the window was a house, and there was a window in that house too, right opposite, and in that window you could see a fat old woman looking out, eating plums and spitting the stones straight out of the window onto the sidewalk. You could see her there at the window so often that looking at her you could imagine that that was how she lived, never leaving the window for a minute.

And, looking out of the window, I thought of the Boy and that he had no idea of windows whatsoever (there couldn't be any windows in a tightly sealed spaceship); instead of windows he had the screen, but it couldn't fully take the place of a window. And then I thought that windows are wonderful things. You could look out into the distance from a window, as if there weren't any walls in the building, and see the clouds and trees and the old woman eating her plums. I asked Starovertsev if he had any notes on his cards about windows and in what century or millennium the window had first made its appearance.

The question seemed to confuse him somewhat and he said that he hadn't filled in that card yet.

'Why?' I asked.

'Because the window was an invention of ancient eras,' he answered. 'I am filling my cards with data which only concerns the future.'

'Won't there be any windows in the future?' I was interested to know.

'Sure there will, but they will be different. Say, for instance, that you won't see a barber shop or a cobbler's shop through your window in the future, but a piece of the universe. That's what the windows will probably be like in future.'

Gromov was listening to what we were saying but he made no remarks although I could see from his face that the question of windows had caught his interest. But he was too tactful to break into the conversation as he had no need to mess around with cards or reference books to find out in which century or millennium man had hewed through his wall to make the first window. Gromov assuredly knew all about that.

The question bothered me but I kept from asking Gromov. I was being tactful too. Many of the kids were irritated because Gromov knew so much, especially those kids who couldn't check up on what he told them and had to take him at his word. They also considered that Starovertsev was envious of Gromov and that he wanted to catch up with him with the help of his cards. All the tables and desks in his apartment were covered with boxes filled with those cards. He was like some professor who didn't trust the encyclopedia or his own memory. It might have been so, but Starovertsev hadn't managed to catch up with him or even come near to it. The kids asked me and Vlassov if Gromov had boxes of cards at home. But I had never seen a single card or box at his house except the box his mother grew flowers in during the summer time. Anyway, everyone came to the conclusion that Gromov just had an amazing memory.

I don't know whether it was his memory or something else, but when Gromov answered a teacher's question something extraordinary seemed to take place in the world – everything around us seemed to change, we changed and the teacher changed and it seemed to us that an unseen cable existed that connected Gromov with the moon and the atom and the bottom of the ocean, and the intelligence of the ant or bee and even with Napoleon and Aristotle. And Aristotle and Napoleon and the bees and ants and the moon and the bottom of the ocean all seemed to associate with him. They all seemed to have confidence in him, and told him everything. One of the kids in class even produced a hypothesis that the Boy in the story really existed and helped Gromov with advice. A lot of the kids began to laugh at this hypothesis and Starovertsev asked:

'How many million years has he existed?'

Some of the kids even defended the hypothesis. Dorofeyev, our top pupil, said that it could be possible that Gromov's father had found the Boy's informative double. He had read about such things in science-fiction books. To be short, Gromov was not connected with the Boy himself, but with his double. The inner life of the Boy had been taken down in code and the Boy's double life in Gromov's apartment, and the real Boy had disappeared long ago having been subjected to the inevitable law of deterioration.

I thought this hypothesis was extremely naïve. And then I didn't think it would have been very ethical of Gromov's father to conceal this informative double of the Boy from science and society just for his son's success at school. This was my first argument against the hypothesis. I had many others. How could the double of the Boy know about such things, say, as Napoleon, and many other things which could not have existed on that planet. Reason and logic resisted in every way, but stronger than these feelings was the feeling and wish to be a witness and participant in extraordinary events. Although I reproached myself for inconsistency, the thought sometimes entered my head: what if Gromov's Boy really existed? Of course, not really, just his double. But let us just suppose. If so, where was the double? In Gromov's father's study? All right. But if that is so what does it do? Just stands there in the study and talks to Gromov from time to time on science subjects?

But let us drop this fantasy and turn back to reality. Reality was extremely commonplace. I was sick with a fever and had to stay in bed for several days. Starovertsev came to see me. He was afraid of catching the fever from me so he sat in a corner at the other end of the room which my parents still automatically called the children's room, from force of long habit. He sat there, looking over his cards and writing something on them from time to time as if he had completely forgotten about my existence.

'You could have done that at home or at the library,' I told him.

'If I were at home or at the library, I couldn't have been here visiting you,' he retorted.

'I agree with you,' I said, 'but as long as you're here it would be better if you put your cards in your pockets. Can't you get along without them for at least a few moments?'

'I value my time very highly.'

'You can go on valuing it,' I said. 'That's your affair.'

This seemed to have got under his skin and he even dropped some of his cards onto the floor.

When he left I got out of bed and picked up the cards he had dropped. On one of them there were notes on the Cathedral of Notre-Dame de Paris, another was about the ATP molecule and hydrogen links and the third card – I couldn't believe my eyes – was about the Boy's informative double.

Dorofeyev, our top pupil, had been right.

There was a reference on the card to a newspaper item on the findings of Gromov, the archaeologist, and mention was made of the double of a boy who had come from another planet and had lain in the earth ever since the Jurassic formation.

I read and reread the card and my hand was trembling. Then I got back into bed, switched on the light and read and reread it over and over again. Two voices kept up a continuous argument in my brain. One voice said that it was all nonsense, and that Starovertsev had taken it all down from Dorofeyev's words and had dropped them on purpose to make fun of me. The other voice argued that Starovertsev valued his cards too highly to use them that way. The two voices argued and I listened to the controversy not knowing which to give preference to.

The voices argued back and forth putting forward the 'pros' and 'cons' in hundreds. Then one voice began to take over, the voice that talked sense and logic, like our maths teacher, Mark Semyonovich. I pictured Mark Semyonovich in my mind with a piece of chalk in one hand and the blackboard eraser in the other, figures on the blackboard, and his voice dragging out in his perpetual doubting manner, even when there was nothing to be doubtful about.

This voice, the voice of Mark Semyonovich, sat somewhere inside me and argued.

'Let us say,' he said, turning to the class, 'let us say that the existence of the Boy's double is known and we will call it "x". Then, let us ask ourselves why should "y", that is Starovertsev, be in such a hurry to fill in that card which he had kept blank for so long? Let us say that Starovertsev ...'

The voice with the doubting tone went on trying to convince me of something that wasn't very hard to convince me of. Starovertsev wasn't the kind who went in for joking or playing tricks. That meant? That meant that while I was lying here in bed taking my temperature and swallowing pills there must have been an article in the papers about the Boy's double.

I called to my mother who was in the dining-room and asked her to bring me the paper.

'It's Monday today,' she said. 'We don't get the paper on Mondays, and I wrapped the shoes that I took to the repair shop in yesterday's.'

7

I dialled Starovertsev's telephone number. A thick, guttural, masculine voice answered the call.

'I would like to speak to Starovertsev,' I said.

'Starovertsev is speaking,' the voice answered.

I was so upset that I didn't realize at once that I was speaking to Starovertsev's father and was surprised that my school chum should have such a low strange voice over the phone.

'Starovertsev is speaking,' the voice repeated irritably.

'I would like to speak to your son, please.'

'He was taken to the hospital yesterday with an attack of appendicitis.'

Everyone in the world seemed to be in collusion to keep me from getting down to the bottom of the mystery. I lay in bed, swallowed pills, drank quarts of tea with lemon and waited for the doctor from the district polyclinic to come.

The doctor finally came – an old grumpy woman who immediately began complaining that the elevator wasn't in good order. Last time, she said, when she had to go to the sixth floor, the door banged shut behind her and she couldn't get out. She had to shout until the repair man had come to let her out and she had lost forty minutes while she was shut up in the elevator. Today she had walked up without using the elevator as she was afraid of being locked in again and losing time. She rebuked my mother for the elevator, asked her to bring a teaspoon and then made me open my mouth. Then she said I had to stay in bed for at least another two days and went away.

Two days ... I lay in bed two days thinking. I thought of the Boy's double, which Gromov's father had found, if I was to believe Starovertsev's card. Many millions of years had passed since the time of the Jurassic formation, the period when the earth had been inhabited by huge scaly pangolins. That would mean that the double had patiently lain in the earth waiting for reasoning beings that could understand its language and come into association with it to appear.

I wanted to know more about the Jurassic formation and I asked my mother to bring me the textbook on palaeontology that my older brother had used when he was a student. Mother couldn't find that book, but she brought me another book, on the *Palaeontology of Vertebrates.*

I read about a strange fact in the book that almost shook me. It seems that during the Jurassic formation there lived a dinosaur which had small front teeth with very stressed grasping functions and no teeth. This little dinosaur was expert in stealing eggs from big dinosaurs.

The author of the book advanced the theory that from this pangolin with its exceedingly mobile nervous system, had originated the mammals, which meant people too.

I got the idea that if the informative double of the Boy really existed, it would be possible to check up if this hypothesis were true. It seemed to me that it wasn't very fair.

Two days later when I came to school I decided to show Starovertsev's card to Gromov.

I felt as if I had lost the ground from underfoot and was falling down a precipice, but I couldn't help myself; the wish to clear up the mystery was too strong.

Choosing the right moment I pulled out the card from my pocket and silently handed it to Gromov.

I couldn't tear my eyes away from his face, my heart was beating heavily and I became hot, then cold, in turn and I thought my fever had begun all over again. It does happen sometimes.

That minute seemed an hour to me. Then Gromov handed back the card and calmly looked at me.

'Well, what about it? What do you find so surprising?'

'What do I find so surprising?' I exclaimed. 'Do you mean to tell me that the story about the Boy's double has been corroborated?'

'It has.'

'He referred to a newspaper article. Was there anything about it in the newspapers?'

'No. Starovertsev found out from me. He referred to the newspaper to make it look more convincing. He didn't want to indicate that the information had come from a private source. I am the private source.'

The bell put an end to our conversation. Mark Semyonovich entered the classroom, drew a right-angle triangle on the blackboard and began to demonstrate the theorem in that doubting toned voice of his. Tapping his chalk on the blackboard he went on demonstrating the theorem as if he himself didn't believe in what he was trying to prove. Of course it was the fault of the intonation that didn't co-ordinate with the logical argument that ensued from the demonstration.

I wasn't paying attention to what Mark Semyonovich was saying at all. Instead of the theorem I was thinking of the dinosaur that stole eggs from its bigger contemporaries. I couldn't believe that all the mammals had come from that little thief. That meant people too and I didn't want to have that kind of an ancestor. And the only way to find out the truth was with the help of the Boy's informative double found by Gromov's father.

Only the Boy could give the lie to this doubtful hypothesis because he had been on earth during the Jurassic period.

On my way home I thought of the thread that united the mammals with the pangolins through that dinosaur whose front legs were so quick at grasping things. If the dinosaurs had been killed off and become extinct, no mammals would have appeared on earth and neither would have I.

I kept on thinking of that. And again two voices were arguing with each other in my head. One agreed with the hypothesis on the origin of the mammals – the other disagreed.

When I walked into the entrance hall and pressed the elevator button, I found it was out of order. The switch button wouldn't light up. I walked up to the second floor and tried to open the door. But it wouldn't open. There was someone in there waiting to be let out.

'Who's in there?' I asked.

'It's me,' a grumpy woman's voice answered and I recognized the doctor's voice.

'We didn't call you,' I said. 'I'm quite all right.'

'I wasn't coming to see you. It was an emergency call for the Novotelov's on the fourth floor.'

'All right,' I said. 'I'll go upstairs and call the technician.'

I ran upstairs as quickly as I could. I wasn't thinking about the Boy now or the dinosaurs. I was wondering why the elevator always worked when I or my mother or all the other neighbours and their friends used it, and always broke down and played dirty tricks as soon as the old doctor got in. I thought of that and the theory of probability and the theory of games. And then I began thinking about the Boy again.

8

'Do you think I could see the Boy's double,' I asked Gromov. 'I've got to clear up an important question.'

The whole thing sounded extremely stupid and wild. It had sort of been pushed out of the whole rigmarole that was going on in my head.

'What's the question?' Gromov asked calmly, I would even say, indifferently.

So I told him about the dinosaur and its front feet with the grasping function and about the mammals who could hardly stomach the hypothesis connected with the origin of these doubtful animals.

'And you want to ask the Boy's double this question?' Gromov queried.

'Yes,' I said.

'You'll have to wait a while.'

'Why?'

'First of all because you're not the only one who wants to ask that question. Secondly because my father and his assistants have been trying for a long time to decode and understand the language which the Boy thought and spoke in ...'

But here we were interrupted again. The bell rang and the lesson began. I had to wait for the next recess to continue our conversation. The lesson seemed endless ... Finally the lesson was over and I asked Gromov:

'Isn't it possible for me to see him?'

'See whom?'

'The Boy's double.'

'It's quite impossible. It's kept at the Institute of Archaeology and no one can enter except the laboratory assistants.'

'Have you seen him?'

'Allow me to leave that question unanswered.'

I was hurt. His words clearly showed that he didn't trust me.

Gromov could see from the expression on my face that I was hurt. It made him feel uncomfortable and he said:

'Why don't you come over any more?'

'Your apartment is under repairs, isn't it?'

'That was finished long ago. Drop in tomorrow evening. I'll be at home.'

9

There I was standing in front of that padded door with the blue post box on the outside.

I rang the bell and stood waiting. No one seemed in a hurry to open it. Perhaps there wasn't anyone at home?

I pressed on the bell again. Gromov himself opened the door.

'Come in,' he said leading the way into the entrance hall.

'I haven't been here for quite a while,' I said. 'Are your parents at home?'

'My mother's at home, but father's at the Institute. Why?'

'Oh, just like that. Is the idol with the obsidian eyes still on the wall?'

'Sure. You'll see it in a minute. Hang your coat here. Have you seen Starovertsev?'

'How could I? He had his appendicitis cut out a few days ago.'

'Appendix, not appendicitis. He's getting well already and

filling in his cards again. He sent me a whole list of questions ... Come in here.'

We had to pass through the dining-room to get to Gromov's room and I saw the transparent eyes of the wooden idol with its narrow figure, thin hands and little legs, slightly doubled under.

'What were the questions he wanted you to answer?' I asked.

'He's a funny guy, that Starovertsev. He wants me to answer questions that only the Boy or his double could answer. And he demands that I answer them in writing right away, while he's still absent from school.'

'Are you going to answer the questions?'

Gromov looked at me in surprise, but said nothing.

Then I said:

'Have you written any more about the Boy?'

'Yes. I have it somewhere if I can find the copy-book. Everything was in such a mess. It's difficult to find anything since the apartment was repaired. Why?'

'I would like you to read it.'

'No. Sorry, but I'm not in the mood,' he said. 'And then I never like to read out loud.'

'Please, read it,' I begged. 'Please.'

I hated myself for my words and the begging tone, but I kept on at him. I did so want to hear about the Boy before the code was deciphered. That would take a long time.

'Please, read it. It's all the same to you ...'

'No,' Gromov said very decidedly. 'I'm not going to read it. If you like I'll switch on the recorder and we'll listen to the melody which the musician composed, which ... The recording is in father's study. Only don't you tell anybody ...'

He went into his father's study and soon came out carefully holding a record. He turned on the recorder so that I could hear a melody that a musician had composed many million years ago before reasoning and the human ear had appeared on earth.

I listened and the sounds poured forth bright and ethereal. You could hear bits of ice breaking and shattering against each other, you could hear the song of the water as its joyful murmuring melody changed to thunderous sound in its battle against the rocks. This was the unhuman heart of the musician which was beating humanly, and which against all the laws of time and space seemed to be here right next to us.

The sounds poured out and out uniting that which could not be united. They were here, although the dream that had given birth to them was immeasurably far from us.

In the story Gromov had called the one who had managed to come to us, the Boy. And he was a boy who was full of his childhood, although his childhood had lasted for millions of years and had not yet ended.

He was called Boy on the spaceship. And that is what he called himself, too.

Gromov and I were still boys too, but our childhood would soon be over. His childhood went on and on merging with the sounds of the melody that I was listening to.

When the music came to an end I asked a question that probably I shouldn't have asked.

'Did your father find that recording along with Boy's double?'

'Of course not. Where did you get that idea? A friend of my father's composed it. I asked him to.'

'You wanted it to be written by the Boy's musician friend, didn't you?'

'Yes,' I answered softly.

'But the music is nice, isn't it? You liked it, didn't you?'

'Yes. But I would have liked it better if it had been composed by that musician, and then ...'

'When there was still no reasoning or human ear to hear it?' Gromov asked.

'Yes.'

'Can you imagine what the earth was like at that time?'

'I couldn't before . . . But I can now after I heard that melody. Can you imagine what it was like?'

'I don't have to imagine it,' Gromov said. 'I know.'

'How do you know?'

'I am sorry, but permit me to leave that question unanswered.'

10

I permitted him to leave that question unanswered. I just got up and left. I put on my coat in the entrance hall and left. I couldn't stand around and beg any longer.

Someone else in my place probably wouldn't have gone away without finding out the truth. A research worker or big scientist for the sake of science would have sent his sense of dignity to the devil and would have stayed on and gotten to the bottom of things.

But I just got up and left. It's true it didn't make things any easier. I hardly slept the whole night.

The next day something unpleasant happened in class. I don't know why I have called it unpleasant. But it doesn't matter. This is what happened.

We had a new teacher in biology. Our old teacher had retired. Nothing would have happened if our old teacher had been there. You couldn't surprise him with anything.

This new teacher asked Gromov a question. And Gromov answered the question, of course. It wasn't because Gromov answered the question way out of the limits of the programme. It was because Gromov knew what no one knew or could know. And the new teacher understood that at once. I could see that by his eyes. I've never seen such eyes anywhere, neither at the movies nor at the theatre. There didn't seem to be anything else on his face except those eyes. There was everything in those eyes: delight and horror, bewilderment and rage, despair and joy and something else that I can't put into words.

I thought that he must have either fallen ill or gone mad. He began pacing from one corner to the other, as if he had forgotten all about us.

Five minutes had passed and he was still striding up and down the room.

Then he walked up to Gromov.

He said something to him so softly and indistinctly that I could only gather from Gromov's answer what it was all about.

It concerned animals that had become extinct millions of years ago. It wasn't that Gromov gave a very lively and concrete detailed description of them, but he dropped a word that he shouldn't have uttered no matter what, if he wanted to keep everything undercover. When the teacher had disagreed with something he said:

'You know that from the course of palaeontology, but I remember ...'

And he went into one detailed description after another, as if he didn't care two pins about the mystery or the teacher or the top pupil, and that word 'I remember' popped up again ... The teacher seemed turned to stone, unable to utter a word.

I felt sorry for the teacher and still more for Gromov and I shouted out:

'That was just a slip of the tongue!'

The teacher grasped at my words as a drowning man grasps at a straw.

Somehow he managed to bring the lesson to a close. Gromov also quieted down.

11

The new teacher fell ill. He had caught pneumonia. I heard that he had sent Gromov a letter from the hospital. But no one in the class knew what the contents of the letter was. Starovertsev had seen the envelope on Gromov's desk. He knew where it was from and who had written it, from the return address.

I think the teacher must have written to Gromov to explain why he had been so agitated at the lesson. But it didn't need any explaining. I don't know if there was anything about the truth in the letter.

But I thought about it every time I saw Gromov. Then Gromov stopped coming to school too.

There was a rumour that the Gromovs were moving to a science centre near Novosibirsk. Gromov's father had been elected a corresponding member of the Siberian branch of the Academy of Sciences.

I just had to see Gromov before he moved. I kept on waiting for him to come to school, but he didn't. Perhaps he had already arranged all his school papers and wouldn't come any more.

The new biology teacher got well and left the hospital. He acted nervous in class and seemed to be confused. From time to time his gaze would fall on the empty seat near the window where Gromov used to sit. And then a strange expression would appear on his face as if he saw something there that other people couldn't see.

I often glanced at that empty seat near the window too. Through the window I could see the street and the pedestrians on the sidewalk and the window of the house across the road where the fat old woman sat and ate apples or cracked nuts with an iron on the window-sill.

But you could tell from the teacher's eyes that he saw something quite different. Perhaps in his imagination he could see the live and impressive picture of the earth in ancient times. The earth as it was before man and before the mammals appeared upon it, as Gromov had described it.

When I was going home I heard the sound of heels

tapping behind me, someone was trying to catch up with me. I turned around. It was the new teacher.

He caught up with me and we walked side by side for some time without a word.

Then he turned to me and asked:

'What do you think of Gromov?'

'Gromov is moving to Novosibirsk,' I said. 'He's going to live at the science centre there. There's a school there for talented mathematicians and physicists. I suppose he'll be attending that school.'

'Do you think he needs that school?'

'Everyone tries for entrance to that school,' I said, 'but it's hard to pass the exams. I'm quite sure Gromov will be accepted at once.'

'I have no doubt that he will be accepted,' the teacher said. 'But I doubt if he needs that school at all. He knows too much.'

'Yes,' I agreed. 'He knows a lot.'

The teacher's face brightened up. And he bent down and asked me in a trusting tone of voice:

'How does he know so much?'

'Oh, that's simple,' I said. 'His father has a wonderful library.'

'Do you think so?' the teacher said. But from his voice I could guess he wasn't quite satisfied with my answer. But what did he have in mind when he asked me that question? Perhaps he thought that I would tell him everything I knew or thought about the Boy? He certainly wanted a lot.

The teacher took several nervous steps and then said:

'Good-bye,' and turned down Fifth Street.

I praised myself for not having answered his question. But what could I have told him anyway? I didn't know how Gromov got to know so much.

When I got home I took a book that had been given to me on my birthday and began to read it.

Then I looked out of the window. It was snowing. The

snow made the street look new and fresh as if it had just been created. I don't know why but I suddenly began to feel good although I didn't live in a spaceship that was flying to distant planets, but in an ordinary old house that needed repairing badly. And the house was not in any danger of being struck by some meteorite or anything else of the kind. It couldn't miss the track and get lost in the endlessness of the universe. Everything was so commonplace and ordinary. Down in the street across the way I could see the bakery with the old sign over it on which was painted a pretzel, and the dressmaker's shop with the wax dummy of a man in a dumpy-looking suit in the show window, and the telephone booth in front of the shop. A feeling of joy and cosy security filled me as if the next day was a holiday that was going to last a long long time. But then my eye fell on the entrance door of the house across the road where Gromov lived. The feeling of joy and cosiness seemed to have been snapped away by a wild gust of wind. Although it was an ordinary entrance door and an ordinary house it seemed to me that behind that door there existed another world, a world full of adventure and mystery. I stood at the window and wondered at these two worlds and at which one was better: the world with the bakery and dressmaker shop or the one where instead of shops and telephone booths, meteorities flew around.

I thought of the Boy. He had no choice. Fate had chosen for him. He had been born on board the flying spaceship. And his whole life was spent in flying. On the other side of the section where the Boy slept there was no dressmaker shop, there was nothing but void space that was called a vacuum.

I suddenly felt uncomfortable as if I had spoken my thoughts to an audience-filled hall. I began to put on my coat. Exactly one minute later I was standing in front of that padded door again.

I stood in front of it unable to make up my mind and press

the bell button. When I finally got up enough courage to raise my hand the door opened and Gromov's father came out. He had his coat on and was evidently going somewhere.

'He's at home,' he said. 'Go on in.'

I stepped forward. At the moment when I made that step I had no idea what the consequences would be.

Gromov seemed glad to see me.

'Come in,' he said. 'Take your coat off. We've got everything packed already.'

Why he mentioned this I don't know.

When we passed through the dining-room I looked up at the wall, but the idol had already been taken down. It was lying on the floor near a suitcase with its thin little legs doubled under.

And then it suddenly struck me that Gromov was really moving away to another city. Until the moment I had seen the little wooden idol on the floor next to the suitcase I had had my doubts.

When we entered his room Gromov turned to me and asked:

'Have you come over just to see me or on business?'

'On business,' I said.

Gromov didn't ask any more questions. And I couldn't make up my mind to say why I had come.

'Are you taking the skulls along with you?' I asked.

'Yes.'

'And the wooden idol?'

'And the wooden idol too.'

'What about the Boy?'

The word seemed to have sprung out of its own. I would have given a lot to be able to take it back again. Gromov's face underwent an immediate change, as if something had taken him and placed him at a distance. I had the feeling that he wasn't here nearby in the room, but that I was looking at him on the television screen.

'What do you need the Boy for?' he asked in a low voice.

'I want to ask him a question.'

'Go on, ask your question,' he said in the same low voice. 'I'll answer it.'

'I want the Boy himself to answer it.'

'I am the Boy.'

'You?'

'Yes. I am the Boy. Didn't you guess that before?'

I couldn't say a word. I turned cold, then hot, then cold again. Sweat covered my brow.

'Why don't you ask your question?'

'I'll ask it later on,' I said.

'When later on?'

'Next time.'

'But we're leaving for Novosibirsk tomorrow.'

'At what time?'

'Nine o'clock in the evening.'

'Then I'll drop in after dinner, if I may?'

'All right.'

But I didn't go to see him after dinner. I don't know why. Perhaps because I didn't know what I wanted to ask him. I couldn't ask him about the dinosaur that stole eggs from its neighbours. It would have been too petty a question. But I was too upset and too agitated and nothing more serious would enter my head.

12

I remained in this state of upset and agitation for about five or six days, and then it passed away. As soon as it did, oodles of questions that I should have asked the Boy, that is, Gromov, piled up in my head. But Gromov now lived far away in the science centre near Novosibirsk. There was another family living in their apartment now. I saw the furniture van driving up with their things. But they were just ordinary things like tables and chairs and beds and couches. You wouldn't expect to find wooden idols with their legs doubled under or numbered skulls among such things. I watched the furniture men take in the things and my heart contracted with sadness. I thought of the apartment in that house across the road and how different it was when Gromov lived in it, and now other people would be living there – an irreversible process – as Dmitry Spiridonovich our physics teacher liked to say.

I was in a bad mood those days and the kids noticed it.

'What's eating you?' they asked.

'Gromov's gone,' I said.

'So what? What's so important about that? There's someone else in his place now. A new boy. He seems to know a lot too. He's from Gorky. He knows three languages.'

There was another boy in the seat near the window. He even looked like Gromov from a distance. He had the same thoughtful look on his face and his hair stuck up straight and stiff like a hedgehog's.

He kept on looking out of the window just like Gromov used to do. Then he made a face and stuck out his tongue at someone. It must have been at the old lady in the window across the road who ate apples and cracked nuts all the time. Gromov would never have done a thing like that. He had treated everyone respectfully and the old lady too.

I certainly wasn't in the best of moods. Those questions that I hadn't asked Gromov kept on bothering me.

The lessons just dragged on and on and when I was going home I saw the new boy walking alongside.

'Do you live far from school?' he asked me.

I told him the name of my street and the number of my house. He was surprised.

'You live right across from my house,' he said.

So I guessed that he lived in Gromov's apartment now. I looked at him and wondered how I felt about him. Whether I could stomach him or not? Again there was an argument going on in my head. One voice said that it wasn't his fault that he now occupied Gromov's seat and had moved into his apartment. The other voice said: sure it's not his fault, but there's something about him. And he's most likely stuck up too.

I decided to ask him a question, one of those that I wanted to ask Gromov.

'Why does the world exist?' I asked him.

'Just because it does,' he answered.

'What would there be if there wasn't any world?' I questioned again.

'We wouldn't be here,' he said.

'That's no answer,' I protested.

'Why do you ask questions like that?' he asked.

'Because I want to know.'

'You want to know a lot, don't you ...?'

'Sure I want to know a lot. Why shouldn't I?'

'Yes, but you ask stupid questions.'

'They aren't stupid at all. You just don't understand, that's all.'

'They are stupid. And then they are not concrete. What sense is there in asking why the world exists?'

'There is sense.'

'There isn't.'

'Gromov wouldn't have answered that way.'

'Gromov? The boy that lived in our house?'

'He didn't live in your house. You're living in his house.'

'We have every right to the apartment, and he left.'

'He didn't leave, he moved to Novosibirsk.'

'So he moved. What's the difference. Do you play table tennis?'

'Sure.'

'Come over to my place after dinner and we'll have a game. We've got a tennis table.'

'I'll see,' I said. 'Maybe I'll come. What's your name?'

'Igor,' he answered importantly. 'Igor Dinayev.'

And again those two voices inside me put up an argument

– whether to go or not. I went. More for the sake of curiosity than anything else.

In the diing-room, instead of the wooden idol, there was a picture on the wall. I couldn't recognize the apartment. The furniture was all new as if it had just come out of the furniture shop. When Gromov lived there the apartment looked something like part of a spaceship. There was hardly any furniture at all. The new furniture and picture on the wall of a bathing beauty with one outstretched long leg touching the water made me feel uncomfortable and out of place. I lost the wish to play tennis and suddenly felt very thirsty. But I thought of the people in the desert who courageously fought against their thirst. So I fought against mine.

'Why don't you say something?'

'I'm thinking,' I said.

'What are you thinking about?'

'About a lot of things.'

'Come on. Tell me!' he demanded.

'I was thinking about the Gobi desert.'

'Were you ever there?'

'No.'

'Then why were you thinking about it?'

'I always think of the places I haven't been to.'

'Then you're a nut. There's something wrong with all the boys in your class. I noticed it at once. Who's the kid you all seem to be harping about?'

'Gromov.'

'What's so wonderful about him? Why does everyone talk about him all the time?'

I changed the subject and began to talk about something else. I didn't want to discuss Gromov with him. And in his apartment too.

Then I got up to go.

'Well, I'll be going. There's a lot of homework to do,' I said.

But there wasn't. As a matter of fact, there was very little homework to do that day.

What else can I say? Hardly anything at all. Everything had become commonplace and ordinary without Gromov in the classroom. But everybody soon got used to it, and began to forget Gromov. I stopped thinking of him all the time too. The homework kept on piling up. We were given so much to do, there was hardly any free time at all. But I still read a lot.

One of the two voices which still argued inside me from time to time said that you couldn't know everything. The other said you could and reminded me of Gromov.

There was no news whatsoever from the science centre near Novosibirsk. I began to think that Gromov had been joking when he said that he was the Boy from the story.

But something happened on Saturday after lessons when I was in the street car with my mother. We were on our way to a housewarming of some friends who had just moved to a new apartment. My mother was holding a huge cake in a white cardboard box on her lap which she had bought at the 'Sever' Bakery Shop. Everything was just as it usually is in a street car. Some people were standing and hanging on to straps, others were seated. One of the passengers was reading a newspaper. I peeped over his shoulder and glanced at the third column and the letters began to jump all over as if I were looking at them through my father's glasses. But still I managed to read the following:

'A profound study is being made of the informative doubles of people who visited the earth during the Jurassic period of formation discovered by Professor Gromov. The Professor's fifteen-year-old son has greatly helped the scientists in studying the possibility of human perception of the psychology and knowledge of the double of the boy who came to earth from another planet. The memory reserves appeared to be extraordinarily vast...'

The words danced up and down before my eyes. I turned cold, then hot, then cold again.

'What's the matter with you?' my mother asked.

I had no time to answer. I dashed after the man with the newspaper who had stood up and was hurriedly making his way towards the exit.

'The paper!' I shouted at the top of my voice. 'Please let me have that newspaper!'

Anatoly Dneprov

THE PURPLE MUMMY

You know the feeling you get when you come to the Capital. It is as if you've just dropped into a new world. As helicopters transfer you from one square to another, or as you skim over the tops of huge palaces in gyroplanes that glide noiselessly along on powerful cables, or just as noiselessly descend into the underground railways streaming with bright sunlight whose source is a mystery, it seems that everything that is striking and unique, everything that points to the future, is concentrated in this amazing and ancient city of Moscow.

I don't consider myself a hopeless yokel. In the north where I live, in the city of Leninsk, we too have got suspension cableways, helicopters and TV information centres in all the big squares. Nevertheless, when I am in Moscow I go about with a slight feeling of confusion and awe. I often wondered why, and finally came to the conclusion that it was because of the accelerated tempo. Life pulsates much faster in the capital. Even the people, who are very hospitable and warm by nature, always seem to be in a hurry. They don't stand still on the moving sidewalks, but almost run as they are carried along. They seem to be trying to keep up the traditions of their forebears who used to rush down the noisy escalators of the old Moscow Metro, several decades ago, and even managed to read at the same time.

I stopped at the TV information centre on Vostania Square, which is suspended high between the two huge buildings of the Sports Palace and the Palace of Art, and dialled the address of the Museum of Material Culture, the place I was making for. The necessary co-ordinates flashed onto the screen along with directions as to how to find my way to the museum.

I was to descend to the lower park and board a winged reactor-plane which would take me to the Monument of Freedom on the Friendship of Peoples Canal. From there I was to transfer to a helicopter and land on the Blue Way which led straight to the museum through the Agate Tunnel. The colour screen showed a thirty-storied building in the shape of a parallelopiped, inlaid with orange ceramics and a fifty-metre bas-relief in snow-white marble of the first space rocket we had launched to the moon. I set out in the direction indicated and in less than a hundred and thirty seconds had reached my destination. On the way I used my private automatic radio-telephone to inform Professor Sayen of my arrival. He met me at the museum entrance.

'Glad to see you, my young friend!' he exclaimed in his melodious voice as he welcomed me and grasped my hand in both of his. 'What brings you to this quiet corner of ours in this ever-bustling city?'

I looked attentively into the slightly mocking eyes of this scientist who was no longer young and recalled how he had looked two years ago when I was taking my post-graduate course at the Revolution University near Moscow. He hadn't changed.

'I'm afraid I have chosen an inopportune time for my visit,' I said. 'The radio news said that you are getting ready to leave for Togo ...'

'Not in the least, not in the least!' the Professor protested. 'I still have thirteen hours at my disposal. I am quite sure that will be more than sufficient to clear up your problems.'

'I don't think it will require more than two or three hours of your valuable time,' I said. 'Perhaps, if you don't mind, we could begin at once ...'

I had no idea how mistaken I was.

We entered a marble hall and a noiseless elevator shot us

up to the museum's seventeenth floor where Professor Sayen had his office. On our way up the Professor told me something about the programme of their trip to Togo ...

'We are in need of additional information on the second stage of the independence struggle of the people of that district. Many years have passed and no one has as yet gone through the archives ... it's one of the weak spots in our museum,' he concluded bitterly. 'Well, I am at your disposal,' he said, seating himself on the couch.

I made myself comfortable in an arm-chair, opened my brief-case, took out a photograph of Maya, my wife, and handed it to the Professor.

'Is this face familiar to you?' I asked, watching closely to catch the slightest movement of the muscles in his tired face.

Professor Sayen took a quick glance at the photograph, puckered his brows and turned his eyes towards me in bewilderment. He seemed to be thinking hard, but shook his head. Back in Leninsk, as I was saying good-bye to my wife, she had said: 'You just watch ... he'll do this ...' And she had shaken her head, puckered her brows and pouted her lips, exactly as the Professor was doing at the moment.

'No, I can't say that I do,' he answered quizzically, looking at me.

He was somewhat taken aback when I nodded with satisfaction and began rummaging about in my brief-case. This time I pulled out the latest edition of the Museum's catalogue. The Professor grew impatient and moved closer to where I sat.

'Could you tell me what this is?' I asked, as I handed him the catalogue opened at the page with the inset of the portrait of the purple mummy.

It does happen that the editor-in-chief of a big publication is not always aware of everything that is printed in it. He is as human as the next man and it is quite natural that he pays more attention to material connected with his own field. His assistants answer for the rest. It is most probable that is what had happened in this case.

Professor Sayen took another look at the portrait of the mummy and turned over several pages of the catalogue to make sure of the name of the museum's new exhibit. Suddenly he exclaimed:

'Why, it's one and the same thing!'

'What is?' I asked, anticipating what was coming next.

'The picture of the purple mummy and this!' he said in wonderment.

'I knew that's how it would be,' I said, and placed the portrait of my wife next to the inset in the catalogue.

'Knew how what would be?' he queried in a puzzled voice.

'I knew that was what you would say. I had an argument with Maya. She was sure you would notice the difference at once.'

Professor Sayen's face took on a stern expression.

'I do not understand you. Whatever are you talking about? Who is this Maya that you have mentioned?'

'I was talking of the likeness of the photograph. Maya is my wife.'

'What has your wife got to do with this?'

'The photograph is of my wife, and this,' I said, pointing to the inset, 'is a picture of the purple mummy.'

The Professor sprang up from the couch and looked me up and down. I noticed that his brows were quivering slightly.

'I hope you have not travelled five thousand kilometres just for the sake of a joke?' He spoke with evident restraint.

I could see that he was finding it difficult to keep his voice in check.

'Not in the least. As a matter of fact it is this likeness that has brought me here. You are aware that I head the Museum of Regional Studies in Leninsk. When I received this edition of your catalogue I was astounded at the likeness between my wife and the purple mummy...'

He took the catalogue out of my hands and approached the broad window. It was about noon and bright daylight streamed in through the scarcely perceptible thin glass. A helicopter flashed by, but the professor didn't take the slightest notice. He was preoccupied in making a thorough comparison of the two portraits.

I recalled Maya's words: 'He'll say that there is a difference in the shape of the neck.'

'Why, the shape of their necks is different!' Professor Sayen cried out joyfully.

I went up to him and smiled.

'That is true. Their necks are not alike. But their faces are exact copies of each other. Just now I am interested only in the likeness. The differences may be gone into later on ...'

We sat down again where we had been before. I chose the armchair and the Professor sat on the couch.

'Tell me more about what brought you here,' he requested.

I was a little nervous because the most important moment had arrived: I had to make myself as clear as possible. I pressed my lips together and my gaze wandered uneasily around the spacious study trying to find an object that would help me begin my story.

'Look at the bust of Academician Philio in the left corner behind his desk,' I recalled Maya's admonitions.

I finally located Philio's bust and began turning the pages of the catalogue. Finding the page I was looking for I showed it to the Professor.

'Look,' I said, 'do you know who this is?'

'That's Philio,' Professor Sayen answered without the slightest hesitation. 'I would like to know what you are driving at. What sort of guessing game are you playing?'

It was now my turn to show impatience. I glanced at the clock. Our short talk was certainly becoming quite a drawn-out affair. Another helicopter flashed by the window. That meant another five minutes had passed.

'Excuse me, Professor, but no doubt you do not read all the material that is published in your catalogue.'

He bunched his hands together nervously. It appeared that the idea I was trying to convey had just got through to him. Why had Philio's bust been placed in the catalogue of the Museum of Material Culture?

He gave a confused smile and passed his hand lightly over his forehead.

'You know, I never noticed that ... I did see it of course, but I didn't pay any special attention to it. It concerns the department of radio-astronomic information and I suppose ...'

Professor Sayen suddenly stopped talking and turned pale. He began to get up slowly from the couch, his wide-open eyes glued to my face. 'What has all this got to do with Academician Philio?' The question blazed out of his frightened eyes.

'Let me see that catalogue again,' he whispered.

With the catalogue grasped tightly in his hand he crossed the study at a diagonal, nearly banging into his desk, and came to a dead stop in front of the bust of the famous linguist.

A strained silence reigned in the room for several seconds. Then the Professor switched on the dictaphone.

'I would like to see Androv in my study at once . . .'

The timbre of his voice was soft, but a slightly menacing note betrayed itself. He picked up the telephone receiver and spoke into it:

'Is that you, Aginov? Who edited Androv's stuff for the last number of our catalogue? Who checked it with the original? Are you sure? Who did the photography job? Thank you.'

The Professor had forgotten about my presence. He sat down at his desk and fell into a deep study of the portrait in the catalogue.

Suddenly he remembered me.

'Give me the portrait of that girl ...'

'Which girl?'

'The one you showed me.'

'You mean Maya?'

'I don't know what her name is ... Let me have it ... quickly ...'

'It's a photograph of my wife,' I put in determinedly.

'That is of no importance ...' He cut me short.

He stared at both portraits for a long time with his head between his hands.

The door opened and a tall middle-aged man dressed in a light yellow sports suit came in. He strode briskly towards the Professor's desk.

'Is this your work?' Professor Sayen asked without lifting his eyes.

'Yes.'

'Aren't you ashamed of yourself?'

'I don't understand what you mean ...'

'You will understand in a moment. Look!'

Sayen nearly threw the picture of my wife into Androv's face.

'Here is your purple . . . mummy.' Then, directing an enraged glance in my direction he said with biting irony: 'Perhaps this girl of yours ...'

'My wife,' I prompted.

'... this wife of yours is really a ... mummy?'

Androv was staring at Maya's portrait. The Professor looked at him with scorn, contempt written in his eyes.

'In our times ... to have such a thing happen ... such deception ... such cheating ...'

It finally got home to Androv that I was directly connected with all this and he rushed up to me.

'Did you make this mirror-image of my mummy?' he demanded in a menacing voice.

I shook my head. Then, without saying a word he seized my hand and dragged me out of the study. The Professor could hardly keep up with us. Androv switched on a mobile strip of corridor, rushed off to the right and then pushed me into an elevator. We made a headlong descent, ran down another corridor, nearly bumping into the Professor who was making for the same place from another direction, and finally burst into a huge, dimly lighted hall. Quartz sarcophagi were arrayed down the centre and along the walls. We stopped in front of one.

'Look.'

I looked into the sarcophagus and quickly closed my eyes. It couldn't be. It couldn't!

'Look, look!' Androv ordered in a choking voice.

'I'm looking ...' I said, faltering.

'What do you see?' the Professor asked, peering into my face.

'I see Maya,' I whispered, turning my eyes away from the plastic figure of a naked woman.

'Who the devil is Maya?' Androv demanded sharply. 'Are you trying to tell me that you know this creature?'

A deadly silence ensued. I was the first to find my voice.

'Excuse me, but that is a model of Maya, my wife ...'

Androv burst into peals of laughter and shouted:

'Take a good look, perhaps you can find some special birth marks on the body of your wife!'

He put an acid stress on the words 'your wife.'

I took another look at the woman's figure lying there with wide open eyes as if she were alive ... The plastic material that she was made of was purple. The most improbable thoughts were racing around in my head. I thought I was going mad.

'Everything seems to be the same except the colour of her body ...'

This was followed by another burst of mocking laughter.

'Oho! So it's the colour! So she isn't quite like your wife!'

There was the same malicious stress on the words 'your wife'... I felt highly embarrassed.

I cast a pleading look in Androv's direction. These learned men from the capital often disregard the most elementary rules of etiquette and stop at nothing to prove their point.

'I really have nothing against this being here,' I said, 'although you should understand ... Well, it's a good thing that you've only got a picture of the head in your catalogue, and ...'

'Did you hear what I heard? Did you hear what he just said? He's got nothing against this thing being here! Do you have any idea what this thing is? My God, this is one of the greatest discoveries ever made! Four of the most powerful radio-telescopes were in continuous operation for more than a hundred hours so as not to miss the slightest signal! The information received was decoded simultaneously both in Moscow and Paris! The best machines we have were used to convolve all that information to achieve this! And you say ...'

This passionate flood of words was interrupted by Professor Sayen.

'Was the head of Academician Philio also convolved in Moscow and Paris?' he interjected in a stern sharp voice.

Androv stopped short and stood frozen to the spot, his mouth open.

'What Philio?' he finally managed to get out.

'This one.'

The Professor pivoted us to a quartz cowl which stood in the centre of the hall. I recognized a copy of the bust which stood in the Professor's study. This one was made of plastic material and was also purple in colour.

Androv nodded his head.

'Well, say something!' the Professor demanded.

'Yes ... we used the same machines for both of them ... we ...'

'Who do you mean by "we"?'

'I, that is, the whole space radio-information decoding department ... you know ... behind the Pantheon ... over there near the ...'

Androv stopped short. He looked at us wild-eyed.

'You don't believe me!' he spluttered.

Professor Sayen shrugged his shoulders. For no apparent reason cold waves began to run up and down my spinal column. A horrible thought was churning around in my brain. At that moment Androv said, almost in a whisper:

'I'm telling the truth. Those two figures were convolved from coded impulse-information we received three months ago from an outlying part of the Swan constellation. We got the information on the head first ... on the twenty-three centimetre band ... Three months later we got the purple mummy on the same wavelength. During reception the noise did not exceed 5db ... the signal-noise ratio was no more than ...'

Suddenly he began to shout: 'That is impossible! What are you trying to do? Who is this Maya? Who the devil is Philio?'

The Professor handed him the photograph of my wife. He compared it to the figure lying in the sarcophagus against the wall ...

'What about Philio? Is he the same man that died three months ago? Did you know him personally?'

The Professor nodded in the affirmative.

Androv jerked to a stop in the middle of the hall as if turned to stone, and then made a sudden dash for the door and disappeared.

With every second I was experiencing a growing feeling of terror. I tried to keep from looking at the transparent lid under which could be seen the purple double of my wife ... The door burst open and Androv returned, accompanied by a woman carrying a small kit bag such as doctors usually lug around with them. Without a word they ran up to the sarcophagus containing the mummy and began taking off the lid.

'What do you intend to do?' Professor Sayen demanded in alarm.

'Dissect it,' Androv whispered, breathing heavily, 'and at once. If what I think is confirmed, then ...'

'What are you going to dissect?'

'The mummy.'

'What for?' I shouted. I had the feeling that they were going to cut up my wife.

At that moment the woman took a scalpel and a disc-shaped electric saw out of her bag.

'I won't allow you to do this! This is valuable public property and you have no right to destroy it without getting permission from the International Science Council,' Professor Sayen stated categorically. 'Besides I do not see any sensible reason for treating this exhibit, which has been acquired from space with such difficulties, if it really has been acquired from space, in the manner you propose.'

'Don't let that bother you, Professor. All the data has been recorded on electret cylinders. She can be reconstructed any time. It would take no more than a day or two. Anthonia, get to work.'

He spread his arms wide, barring the way to the sarcophagus. I heard the whining sound of the saw as it bit into the mummy. Ice-cold waves followed each other up and down my spine.

'Now dissect the chest,' Androv commanded. 'Holy Moses, can't you saw any quicker! Are you through? Now turn back the breast-bone. Have you found the heart? Aha! Where's the liver? That's right! And the spleen. That's all. Now we can let them see it.'

Androv grabbed my shoulder.

'What are you afraid of? It's only a mummy made of plastic. Somebody's double. An exact copy. You can see for yourself how well the copy has been made ...'

I approached the sarcophagus reluctantly. Parts of the dissected plastic body were spread back symmetrically from its centre and its internal structure was clearly visible. The organs were of different colours, but all with a purple tinge ... The mummy's eyes were wide open and didn't express the slightest sign of suffering. It cost me a great mental effort to convince myself that this was not a live organism, but just a cleverly made copy of a human being.

'Is this a copy or isn't it?' Androv demanded as he grabbed my shoulders and shook me. His eyes shone with ill-concealed joy. 'Take a good look at it!'

I nodded my head dejectedly.

'What is your opinion, Professor?' Androv asked eagerly.

He was answered by a cry from the woman who had dissected the mummy.

'Everything is the wrong way round!'

I stared at her wide-eyed, trying to understand what she had said.

'What do you mean, Anthonia?' the Professor asked hoarsely.

'Everything! Her heart, liver, spleen ... they're all the wrong way round!'

Finally I understood. The mummy's heart was on the right side and its liver on the left, as if it were a reflection in a mirror!

'Do you realize what we have achieved! This is colossal confirmation of the theory of Anti-Worlds. This is staggering news! This ...'

'Will you please explain what you are talking about!' Professor Sayen demanded.

This remark reminded Androv that we were there. He walked away from the mummy, embraced the Professor, and said, solemnly:

'At last we have experimental proof that somewhere in the depths of the Universe there exists an anti-world which is an exact copy of ours but composed of anti-matter. Such a world might be considered as an inverted image of ours.'

2

As I made my way to the Palace of Science along the swiftly moving platforms and thoroughfares of the capital, here and there above the general restrained hum and buzz of voices I could hear the words: 'Purple Mummy, Purple Mummy ...'

After the International Council of scientists had made a special announcement concerning Andronov's astounding and, to say the least, bold hypotheses, it was the talk of the whole world, let alone Moscow. A new copy of the mummy was put on exhibit at the Museum of Material Culture in place of the one that had been dissected. The influx of visitors from many cities in other parts of the world became so great that several copies had to be made. They were put on exhibit in the largest public halls of the capital. By special order of the Supreme Council, the portrait of the mummy was relayed three times a day on the stereo-television colour screen. Moscow echoed with 'the Purple Mummy, the Purple Mummy.' My head buzzed with something quite different: 'Maya ... Maya ... Could there be, somewhere in the Universe, another woman exactly like my wife?'

I could stand it no longer. In a quiet corner of the Kremlin Park I pulled my radio-telephone out of my pocket and dialled Leninsk. A few seconds later I heard the drawn out sound of the buzzer.

'Is that you, Maya?'

'Yes. What's all this excitement about the Purple Mummy? I think I am going to invoke the law of respect for personal dignity in protest against being put on show for the whole world to see!'

This was my Maya – a very vital and effervescent little woman. A weight fell from my shoulders as I listened to her bell-like, bantering voice.

'Don't be silly. You ought to be proud of yourself!' I countered.

'I am! The press, the radio and television over here are leading me a merry dance. I have become quite a public figure. You know there was a commission here from Moscow to have me examined! They wanted to make sure that my heart was on the left side!'

'Well, what did they find?'

'Oh, it's on the left side all right! So they know I'm not from the anti-world!' She laughed merrily. 'What are you doing down there?' she asked.

'Keeping my mouth shut and trying to keep in the background. Can you imagine what would happen if they found out that I am the earth-copy husband of that purple lady?'

'They would have to dye you in that horrible colour then! By the way, why have they dyed her purple?'

'Nobody dyed her. That's the way she came out from the information machines. I suppose that's what she should be like according to the rules of the anti-world ... Most people find the mummy quite attractive,' I teased.

'You can stop that. I'm in no mood for compliments! I've had enough of that up here. What are you going to do now?'

I glanced at my watch.

'In eighty seconds I am supposed to be at a conference in the Big Marble Hall of the Academy. I've got to fly.'

'Very well, dear. Good-bye. I'll follow the conference on television. Be seeing you!'

'Good-bye.'

The Marble Hall was packed and I had difficulty in finding a place. I finally found a seat at the back of the hall near the main entrance. I put on the earphones and switched on the screen on the panel of the reading stand. Academician Jonatov, the President of the Academy, made a short speech outlining the aim of the conference, 'to discuss the scientific viability of Androv's hypothesis.' A very stiff time limit was set: each speaker was allowed three minutes at the rostrum and two minutes in the section sittings. These discussions were to be held in the halls of the Academy where sound recorders had been installed, and any delegate could express his opinion and obtain copies of other delegates' speeches or reports.

Androv was scheduled as the fifth speaker. Horner, the radio-astronomist from Chicago, was the first to take the floor. He spoke on the discovery of the sematic significance of the radio signals coming to us from outer space. An equation of the information theory, which was the basis for deciphering signals of a physical nature, appeared on the screen. Horner was followed by Solvin from Moscow, who described the capabilities of the apparatuses which receive signals from the regions of Alpha Swan. Zuggan of Bulawayo spoke on the principles of recording and storing cosmic radio information.

I found the punctilious report of Suzhi, the French radio engineer, the dullest of all. He made detailed observations about ultra-sound spatial scanning of physical bodies and their reverse convolution into models of material information. He said it was based on the same principle as two-dimensional television except that convolution was accomplished with an ultra-sound 'needle', with a sound beam of several microns diameter. In conclusion he said:

'Naturally, to relay information of organisms it is necessary that they be clinically dead, at least for this method of convolution. Ultra-sound beams destroy living cells . . .'

These preliminary reports had been arranged so the delegates could get some idea of the quality of the experimental findings.

Androv finally took the floor.

'I have no intention of repeating known facts relating to elementary particles and antiparticles of matter. I shall just enumerate them: the electron and positron, the proton and anti-proton, the neutron and anti-neutron. The rest of the short-lived particles are of no interest to us. The experiments of Malinovsky and Sague have proved that from elementary particles it is possible to create stable anti-atoms of any element. This is sufficient to build an anti-world. But this is not what I am calling your attention to. Anti-particles are born in pairs. With a certain degree of quantum energy it is possible for atoms to be born in pairs, and, as our latest experiments have proved, paired stars can occur as well as whole planetary systems, one composed of matter and the other of its mirrored antipode – of anti-matter. The pairs that are born are physically alike with the exception of their charge and spin characteristics, as you know. The latter are unable to influence biological evolutionary processes which are conditioned by low energies and weak reciprocal action. I claim that our sun and our planets have their doubles and anti-matter which were born simultaneously from electromagnetic quantums of colossal energy. Such quantums appear from time to time in the Universe as the result of the radiation fluctuation of other stars. If this is so, then there exists an anti-Earth populated by anti-people . . .'

This was followed by a surge of laughter in the hall.

The chairman rose and addressed Androv.

'Anti-people – anti-man – is not a nice expression. It bears an insulting implication.'

'Forgive me. I meant to say human beings composed of anti-matter.'

The laughter subsided.

Androv went on to give a detailed description of the structure of a human being made of anti-matter. He stressed the necessity of inverted symmetry in relation to the Earth structure. When he came to the Purple Mummy he became quite carried away and the chairman suggested that he dictate the rest of his report in one of the adjoining halls.

Guton, the next speaker, one of the greatest experts in anthropology, from Novosibirsk, opposed Androv's theory. By using figures he showed how often an amazing likeness could be found between people living in different parts of the Earth. In connection with the inverted situation of the internal organs of the mummy, he also indicated examples of the same phenomena observed on our planet.

Suddenly, upsetting all the rules of decorum, someone shouted from the body of the hall: 'Your probabilities have to be multiplied and will thus decrease by ten orders!'

'Why?' Guton immediately parried the interjection.

'The purple mummy is the exact likeness of an Earth habitant. Secondly, her organs have an inverted pattern. Thirdly, because the bust of a man who is the exact likeness of Philio, the linguist, has also been received from outer space. The coincidence of three extraordinarily complicated events of the same kind is hardly probable!'

Guton wrinkled his brow in thought and remained silent. A murmur of voices swept the hall.

'Go on,' the chairman prompted.

'I don't think I shall. The gentleman has proved his point ...'

Guton stepped down from the platform and took his seat.

I walked out into the lobby and went up to the electronograph which was typing out the first reports of the conference. The speakers were nearby in sound-proof booths.

They argued, opposed, expressed their doubts or tried to refute Androv's hypotheses.

Then I went out onto the open balcony and dialled Leninsk. It was some time before Maya picked up the receiver.

'Aren't you listening in to the conference?' I asked.

'Not at the moment. I feel a bit tired. You know I think Guton is right, even though he did leave the platform. I think the likeness is just a coincidence. There are a lot of coincidences of that kind on our planet, and throughout the Universe as a whole they must be quite inevitable. Good-bye, dear. I think I had better go and lie down again ...'

Maya replaced the receiver and I had no chance to tell her that I would have preferred the Purple Mummy to have been like someone else ...

3

The worst began after the conference was over. The delegates had left for their respective cities, having come to the unanimous conclusion that the experimental data supporting Androv's hypotheses were insufficient. In a matter of hours the world lost interest in the Purple Mummy. Its doubles were removed to the basement of the museum and only the one that Androv had dissected was taken down to the Central Anatomical Theatre.

Anatomists, pathologic-anatomists, physiologists and cytologists still worked on the mummy. Before leaving for Leninsk I decided to go and see if anything new had been discovered, and bumped into Androv in the doorway of the dissecting department. He seemed to be in a state of extreme exhaustion.

I looked in through the partly open door and saw several doctors bending over the shapeless remains of the Purple Mummy.

'How are things?' I asked Androv.

'Fair. We have proved that there is no doubt about the symmetrical inverted structure of the internal organs ...'

'In that case what are they doing with her now?'

Androv shrugged his shoulders carelessly.

'They are trying to discover the mummy's age from that model in order to compare it with the age of your wife.'

'It's a pity the people of the Anti-world didn't attach a sheet of paper containing her biography when they sent her over here by radio,' I joked. 'We would have managed to read the inverted reflection of the letters, I'm sure.'

'I'm sorry about something else. My opponents would have had a harder time proving their points if I had managed to receive Professor Philio's whole body and not just the head ...'

I nodded in agreement.

'Your wife worked with Philio, didn't she?'

'Yes. She was his assistant. She studied the Indonesian group of languages under his guidance.'

Androv nodded his head.

'There is another way to prove that my hypothesis is right ... but it all depends on them ...' He nodded in the direction of the dissecting department.

'The mummy's age?'

'Yes, and several other things ...'

Androv took my elbow and led me along the corridor.

'There's nothing interesting in there at the moment. Would you like me to show you how the machine works that convolves the models from the spatial scanning of the originals?'

'You bet!'

An escalator took us to the top airway where we boarded one of those noiseless cable-born gyroplanes and were transferred from one end of Moscow to the other in a few minutes. The sky was blue, cloudless and cold. The city was a mass of green and seemed to be covered with a bluish haze.

'Were you born here?' Androv asked me.

'No,' I answered.

'During the last thirty years our city has seen the most amazing changes.'

'That's true,' I agreed. 'I say, what other things besides the age of the mummy can help you to prove your theory?'

Androv hurried on, taking no heed of the interruption, as if he wished to avoid answering my question.

'I have lived here ever since I was born and the second reconstruction of Moscow took place right in front of my eyes. It all happened like in a fairy tale . . .' These giant palaces and parks seemed to spring up from nowhere. In place of the Metro we have these noiseless machines and helicopters circling over the city. The network of wires for trolley buses and trams has gone and now there are these suspension bridges over a hundred metres high, and these towers of shining metal that the gyroplane cables are attached to . . . Life has become so thrilling, so wonderful. Life has become so wonderful ...' he repeated thoughtfully.

I wanted to repeat my question, but at that moment the gyroplane came to a stop in front of a platform.

'Well, here we are,' Androv said. 'That's our receiving centre over there.'

I looked down upon a small building with a flat roof covered with green twining ivy.

The machine that created the plastic volumetrical models on the bases of their pulsed scanning was called an electronic-acoustic repeater. It was a huge structure of shining stainless steel and blinding white enamel. Now and again a stream of warm or cooled air shot out from the cooling channels, and a hardly perceptible hum came from the machine.

Behind a glassed partition, at the end of the hall, there was another machine much smaller than the first. We went towards it.

A girl sat at the control panel reading a book. From time to time she lifted her eyes from the book and looked at the panel. A neon light in front of her went on and off at irregular moments.

'What have you got at the moment, Galya?'

'The model of a new atom reactor. From Rome,' the girl answered, rising.

'By radio or cable?'

'By radio-relayed line.'

Androv nodded and turned to me.

'Take a look and see how it's done. Here's where we receive the code information in which the co-ordinates of every point of the object being sent is ciphered – along with the colour of the material the object is made of, its constructive details, its thickness, length and so on. From the amplifier the impulses enter the decoder. After they are fed into different channels they activate the relay which operates the mechanical and chemical parts of the machine.'

We returned to the machine in the big pavilion and approached a huge mirror-like show-case in the centre. Androv turned on the light and the interior chamber was brightly illuminated. A shapeless mass stood in the chamber with thin metal needles touching it on all sides.

'This is where the information is convolved into the model of the object. These thin air-cooled needles are something like those used for intermuscular injections. A thin stream of plastic material is pressed through them in short spurts. The needles are synchronized with the ultra-sound needles which are at this moment feeling around the real object. Drop by drop, from point to point, the thin stream of plastic builds the model. The scale of the model may be regulated by using these levers. They may be made larger or smaller than the real object ...'

'What about the colour?'

'That's easy. In the initial state the material is colourless, but the photo-calorimeter, according to the colour information received, introduces the necessary amounts of the dyes indicated ...'

'So this is where the Purple Mummy was born?'

Androv nodded.

'Nevertheless, I still can't understand why it is purple. If everything is as you say, it should be flesh-coloured . . .'

'There was a great deal of controversy on the subject at the conference. I think one of the physicists came up with the correct explanation to this puzzling phenomenon. Have you ever heard of the Doppler effect?'

'Isn't that where the length of the light wave increases if the source of radiation recedes from the observer?'

'Exactly. For example, you can recede at such a great speed that for the stationary observer the colour of your body will appear to be red. I think that the colour of the mummy indicates that the anti-world is moving in the opposite direction to our planet at a terrific speed...'

At that moment the girl called out to him from behind the glass partition:

'You are wanted on the telephone!'

Androv excused himself and I stood there watching the needles exude plastic as they produced a volumetrical reproduction of an object that was located tens of thousands of kilometres away. I tried to picture how excited the scientists must have been as they watched the needles drawing the volumetrical figure of a human body which was located at a distance exceeding all imagination.

Androv rushed up to me and seized my shoulder.

'Come on! Quick! We've got to hurry!'

'Where to?' I exclaimed with surprise.

'Back to the anatomical theatre as quickly as possible...!'

With absolutely no idea what it was all about I hurried after him. We soared up to the gyroplane line and at last came to a stop.

'What has happened?' I asked.

'When did you last speak to your wife?'

'What do you mean...?'

'When did you last speak to your wife?' he repeated, staring at me with his deep black eyes.

The gyroplane set off. Androv pulled me inside and opened the porthole. A strong gust of air blew in.

'Take out your radio-telephone and get in touch with your wife at once.'

I pulled the apparatus out of my pocket.

'Let me see it. Oh dear, it's got a ferrite antenna. That's bad... Well, try to stick it out of the porthole as far as you can and use the phone. The hull of the gyroplane is made of metal and will guard your apparatus from radio-eradiation.'

I pressed myself up against the porthole as much as I could and dialled Leninsk. My heart was beating furiously. What was it all about?

'Well?'

'There's no answer . . .'

'Try and stick the apparatus out a little further.'

I dialled the number again.

'There's no answer . . .' I said hoarsely.

'Here . . . give it to me . . . I'll hold it out as far as it will go and you listen.'

Androv took the radio-telephone and stuck his arm out of the porthole up to his elbow. At that moment the speed of the descending gyroplane increased sharply, something jerked, and the telephone flew out of my hand.

'Damn! Now we can't do anything!'

My apparatus had been blown away by a powerful current of air. Androv had banged his arm against the porthole and it was bleeding just below the elbow.

For a short period we stared at each other in silence. There was a look of horror in his eyes.

'What has happened to my wife?' I finally managed to squeeze out in a whisper.

'I don't know . . . we'll find out right away . . . Try and remember exactly to the day how old your wife is and exactly how much time has passed since the day of Philio's death.'

My brain was in an awful muddle . . . I couldn't have solved the simplest sum in arithmetic. Besides, I couldn't make out what he wanted and why. Finally I managed to blurt out:

'My wife is twenty-three years, three months and six days old . . . Philio died three months and three days ago . . .'

'Have you included the leap years?'

'No.'

'Never mind. I'll do it. Tell me the day, month and year . . . No, you better just tell me the date of Philio's death . . .'

The gyroplane came to a stop softly. Androv took hold of

my hand and towed me along to the exit, muttering something under his breath as we ran.

We said nothing all the way to the anatomical theatre. I couldn't remember anything. I had forgotten the date when Maya was born. I couldn't recall when Philio had died.

We were met in the lobby by a doctor who was smiling happily. He was holding a big chunk of purplish-orange plastic in his hands. Androv put his finger to his lips as a sign that he should keep quiet, but the doctor paid no heed.

'I can almost congratulate you, I can almost congratulate you!' he exclaimed.

'All that's necessary now is to find out what our Earth habitant died of! We know what the Purple Mummy died of. Look!' He handed Androv the plastic lump he was holding. 'Lymphosarcoma! A wonderful plastic model of the tumour!'

I reeled backwards in horror.

'What did you say?' Androv shouted.

'Nothing much. I certainly am surprised that on that anti-world of yours they don't know how to treat a simple thing like that. They've learned how to send the corpses of their people to us by radio, but they haven't thought of a way to treat tumours! It's a real shame.'

The doctor's face took on a scornful expression as he turned and walked towards the dissecting room in a slow and dignified manner. I had difficulty in moving my feet. My brain was in a whirl trying to imagine what could have happened to Maya. The five thousand kilometres to Leninsk took on cosmic proportions. My heart contracted with pain ...

'How old was she when she died? I mean the Mummy,' Androv called out.

'Kugel will tell you. But what I can't understand is why they didn't cure that woman. Of course, sometimes neoplasm doesn't give any indication of its presence until the last moment. The only symptom is a slight feeling of tiredness, and that's all. You know what our young people are like. They wouldn't think of paying attention to a thing like that. They don't give a hoot about medical aid. And you see what comes of it ...'

The doctor's voice sounded loud and harsh as if he were talking through a megaphone.

We entered the dissecting room. An elderly man who was not wearing a smock was seated at a marble-topped table making some sort of calculations in a note-book.

'Kugel, what is your estimate of how long she lived?' the doctor asked, and pointed at the mutilated plastic figure.

'Eight thousand, five hundred and twenty-three and a half days. I'm not quite sure of the half,' Kugel said, as he went on calculating.

'Doctor,' said Androv, 'this is her husband ...' He gave me a light shove in the direction of the doctor.

'Whose husband? Her husband?' he asked, indicating the sawn-up bits of plastic.

'Wonderful! He can tell us the exact day when his wife died. Do you remember?'

At that moment I was thinking about something quite different. I remembered the report made at the Conference by Suzhi, the French engineer. He had said that the volumetrical convolution of an organism is possible only after death. I remembered, too, that there had been an interval of three months between the reception from outer space of the mummy and Philio's bust. Philio had died three months ago ... perhaps today might be the exact day when the three months were up?

The doctor repeated his question in a honeyed tone, as if he were talking to a patient. I shook my head.

'You don't remember? You don't remember when your wife died?' The doctor sounded surprised.

I had lost the ability to speak. Androv answered for me.

'It is quite possible that she has not died. He was talking to her over the radio-telephone only two hours ago ...'

'Not died? That is impossible!' the doctor stated categorically. 'I have infinite confidence in your theory of the existence of an anti-world, Androv. That is why she, that is, his wife, has to die. Otherwise we have no way of proving the existence of the anti-world and our anti-doubles out there,' he raised his eyes to the ceiling, 'in the Universe ...'

I nearly choked with rage. Menacingly I went for the doctor who was carried away with enthusiasm.

'Hold your tongue! I don't give a damn about your anti-world! She isn't dead. And if she is ill she has to be treated at once!'

Androv held me back.

'Calm down. Calm down, will you. I'll have Leninsk on the air in a minute. Come on.'

As if in a dream I walked down corridors, flew along streets, went up in elevators, listened to voices speaking ...

'What was the wavelength you used to contact your wife?' I heard a voice asking.

'I don't know ...'

'What is your telephone number?'

'I don't remember ...'

'What is your name?'

I told them.

'Sit down here.'

Androv sat down beside me and put his hand on mine.

'They'll find her right away, don't worry ...'

I nodded. A deep silence reigned in the room. A huge pendulum clock ticked in front of me. I dimly perceived a big palm tree in a wooden barrel and Lenin's bust to the right of it on the wall. The bust was made of red marble. The clock kept on ticking – very slowly.

Then someone said:

'Go into booth number three.'

I still sat as if turned to stone. No feelings, no thoughts ...

'Go into booth number three,' the voice repeated.

'Go on in. They've contacted Leninsk,' Androv said, pulling at my sleeve.

I went out. Booth number three ... there it was. And there was the telephone receiver. I picked it up.

I stood there in silence.

The telephone operator said, 'Go ahead.'

'Maya,' I whispered.

'Hello, hello?' I heard her voice as clearly as if she were standing next to me in the booth.

'Maya!' I shouted, not recognizing my own voice.

'Is that you, Vadim?'

'Maya, are you alive?'

'What?'

'Are you alive?'

'Stop shouting! I can't understand a thing. Why aren't you using your radio-telephone?'

Suddenly my brain became crystal clear. I knew what had to be done.

'Maya, listen carefully,' I began, dragging the words out slowly. 'You are ill. Very ill. Do you understand? Go to the clinic at once and tell the doctor that you suspect you have lymphosarcoma. Go at once, dear. Promise me that you'll go at once!'

My wife's merry, carefree laughter rang out over the telephone.

'How very odd!' she said, finally. 'We have only lived together for four years and we think the same way even with five thousand kilometres between us.'

'Go and see a doctor at once!' I shouted.

'I am speaking to you from the Doctor's,' she shouted back.

I felt an unpleasant sensation deep down in my stomach. She went on speaking in a merry voice.

'You know, I didn't feel very well yesterday. Sort of tired and listless. I went to the clinic today and was thoroughly checked. And what do you think? When I was X-rayed the doctor discovered that the lymphatic glands somewhere near my stomach were slightly swollen. Doctor Eitrov shouted his head off at me. You should have heard him. He said, "You're an educated woman but you come for a check-up so seldom. And now, look, your lymphatic glands are two per cent larger than normal." How do you like that?'

'I like it, Maya,' I said. 'Go on ...'

'Oh, everything was straightforward after that. They gave me an injection and told me to come for another one in six months' time, just to make sure that everything is in order. Isn't that interesting!'

'Very interesting,' I said.

'What are you mumbling about? What happened to the Purple Mummy?'

'She died ... I mean they cut her up. All the other doubles are down in the basement.'

'What about Androv's hypothesis? Did he prove it?'

'I ... I don't know. I'll tell you all about it when I get home.'

'Yes, dear. Come soon. I'm so lonely.'

'I'll be home tomorrow!'

'I'll be waiting for you. Good-bye.'

Androv was all smiles when I walked out of the booth. He threw his arms round me and hugged me to his chest.

For no reason at all I burst out laughing.

'What are you so happy about?' I asked, grinning at him. 'If Maya's lymphatic glands are slightly swollen it doesn't help you to prove your theory of anti-worlds and anti-doubles of people living on Earth.'

'That's not so important. The main thing is that your wife is alive and well. I was very worried.'

'Do you really believe in the existence of an inverted copy of the Earth?' I asked, seriously.

'You believed in it, too,' he said, evasively. 'Otherwise you wouldn't have taken the Purple Mummy's fate so much to heart.'

I smiled in confusion. If you come to think of it, why had I been so afraid for Maya? My wife and the mirrored image sent on through space by radio – what could they have had in common? Nothing, of course!

'If you believe in the existence of anti-worlds, then you must go on deciphering those wonderful signals from the depths of the Universe. Carry on. Perhaps you won't find exactly what you are searching for, but whatever you find will be important ...'

'I'll go on searching,' Androv said thoughtfully. 'So will all the others. But what just struck me is something the doctor who dissected the Purple Mummy said. Do you remember?'

'What was that?'

'Those people out there in the Universe know how to send volumetrical convolution signals, but they don't know how to cure lymphosarcoma ...'

'So what?'

'We've got to send them information on how to cure lymphosarcoma. We've just got to. It's very important for them ...'

'For whom? And where?'

'For the people who sent us the Purple Mummy by radio.'

'But it took those signals millions of light years to reach us!' I protested.

Androv wrinkled his brow and lightly brushed his head ...

Rosemary's Baby 5/-

IRA LEVIN

The book that topped US and British bestseller lists for months and is now a terrifying Paramount picture, starring Mia Farrow, John Cassavetes and Ralph Bellamy.

'At last I have got my wish. I am ridden by a book that plagues my mind and continues to squeeze my heart with fingers of bone. I swear that Rosemary's Baby is the most unnerving story I've read.'
KENNETH ALLSOP, EVENING NEWS

'The pay-off is so fiendish, it made me sweat. Diabolically good.'
PETER PHILLIPS, SUN

'. . . if you read this book in the dead of night, do not be surprised if you feel the urge to keep glancing behind you.'
QUEEN

'a darkly brilliant tale of modern deviltry that, like James' *Turn of the Screw*, induces the reader to believe the unbelievable. I believed it and was altogether enthralled.'
TRUMAN CAPOTE